THE HIDDEN HARBOR MYSTERY

HARDY BOYS MYSTERY STORIES

THE TOWER TREASURE
THE HOUSE ON THE CLIFF
THE SECRET OF THE OLD MILL
THE MISSING CHUMS
HUNTING FOR HIDDEN GOLD
THE SHORE ROAD MYSTERY
THE SECRET OF THE CAVES
THE MYSTERY OF CABIN ISLAND
THE GREAT AIRPORT MYSTERY
WHAT HAPPENED AT MIDNIGHT
WHILE THE CLOCK TICKED
FOOTPRINTS UNDER THE WINDOW
THE MARK ON THE DOOR
THE HIDDEN HARBOR MYSTERY
THE SINISTER SIGNPOST
A FIGURE IN HIDING
THE SECRET WARNING
THE TWISTED CLAW
THE DISAPPEARING FLOOR
THE MYSTERY OF THE FLYING
  EXPRESS
THE CLUE OF THE BROKEN BLADE
THE FLICKERING TORCH MYSTERY
THE MELTED COINS
THE SHORT-WAVE MYSTERY
THE SECRET PANEL
THE PHANTOM FREIGHTER
HARDY BOYS DETECTIVE HANDBOOK

THE SECRET OF SKULL MOUNTAIN
THE SIGN OF THE CROOKED ARROW
THE SECRET OF THE LOST TUNNEL
THE WAILING SIREN MYSTERY
THE SECRET OF WILDCAT SWAMP
THE CRISSCROSS SHADOW
THE YELLOW FEATHER MYSTERY
THE HOODED HAWK MYSTERY
THE CLUE IN THE EMBERS
THE SECRET OF PIRATES' HILL
THE GHOST AT SKELETON ROCK
THE MYSTERY AT DEVIL'S PAW
THE MYSTERY OF THE CHINESE JUNK
MYSTERY OF THE DESERT GIANT
THE CLUE OF THE SCREECHING OWL
THE VIKING SYMBOL MYSTERY
THE MYSTERY OF THE AZTEC WARRIOR
THE HAUNTED FORT
THE MYSTERY OF THE SPIRAL BRIDGE
THE SECRET AGENT ON FLIGHT 101
MYSTERY OF THE WHALE TATTOO
THE ARCTIC PATROL MYSTERY
THE BOMBAY BOOMERANG
DANGER ON VAMPIRE TRAIL
THE MASKED MONKEY
THE SHATTERED HELMET
THE CLUE OF THE HISSING SERPENT
THE MYSTERIOUS CARAVAN

Joe gave a mighty swing, carrying both boys
into the air

Hardy Boys Mystery Stories

THE
HIDDEN HARBOR
MYSTERY

BY

FRANKLIN W. DIXON

NEW YORK
GROSSET & DUNLAP
Publishers

© By GROSSET & DUNLAP, INC., 1961

ALL RIGHTS RESERVED

ISBN: 0–448–08914–9 (TRADE EDITION)
ISBN: 0–448–18914–3 (LIBRARY EDITION)

In this new story, based on the original of the same title, Mr. Dixon has incorporated the most up-to-date methods used by police and private detectives.

PRINTED IN THE UNITED STATES OF AMERICA

CONTENTS

CHAPTER		PAGE
I	THE LIBEL SUIT	1
II	A VANISHING VICTIM	11
III	WATER MONSTER	22
IV	SKIN-DIVING SLEUTHS	30
V	MAROONED!	38
VI	SIGNAL FIRE	47
VII	AMUSEMENT PARK TROUBLE	56
VIII	CAMPFIRE EAVESDROPPER	65
IX	FISHING BOAT CLUE	73
X	HIDDEN PASSAGEWAY	81
XI	ACROBATIC DETECTIVES	89
XII	ALLIGATOR!	99
XIII	HURRICANE	107
XIV	A REVEALING ARGUMENT	117
XV	SEA CITY HOAX	124
XVI	ENEMY TACTICS	132
XVII	UNDERWATER PRISON	140
XVIII	DANGEROUS CARGO	150
XIX	SINISTER ABSENCE	158
XX	FEUD'S END	166

CHAPTER I

The Libel Suit

"Wow! That fellow sure was in a hurry to get past us!" exclaimed Joe Hardy, who had been pushed against the railing of the cruise ship's gangplank.

"Practically knocked us overboard!" agreed his brother Frank.

The two boys, descending the gangplank from the brightly lighted deck, looked curiously after the young man who had shoved them aside.

Joe, fair-haired and seventeen, and dark-haired Frank, a year older, heard the stranger cry out to a deck attendant:

"I tell you, I *must* come aboard!"

"Sorry, sir," was the firm answer. "It's past midnight. We sail at dawn. No more visitors."

The Hardys continued down to the pier. Suddenly they stopped and whirled. The visitor was

1

saying excitedly, "I must see Mr. Hardy before he sails!"

"Maybe it's about a mystery," Frank remarked.

The brothers had just said good-by to their parents, the well-known detective, Fenton Hardy, and his wife Laura, who were leaving from New York City on a Caribbean cruise. Mr. Hardy was making a combination business and pleasure trip, since he planned to see a client in Jamaica.

While Frank and Joe listened intently to the conversation on deck, a powerfully built man came from behind a stack of baggage and sauntered to the foot of the gangway. The Hardys' attention was attracted by the man's heavy, wheezy breathing and his flat face turned upward to the deck.

"All right, all right. I give up," came the dejected voice of the stranger above. As he came down the gangplank, the rough-looking man gave him a swift glance, then shuffled off quickly.

By now the young man had reached the pier. He was slim in build, with reddish-brown hair. Nervously he kept slapping his palm with a rolled-up newspaper, as if in utter frustration.

"Excuse me," said Frank, stepping in front of him. "We heard you mention Fenton Hardy. We're his sons, Frank and Joe."

"You are?" The man's eyes brightened. He had a soft, slow way of speaking that marked him as a Southerner.

"I just about knocked myself out, trying to speak to your father," he continued. "I have a case he *must* handle!"

"He won't be back for ten days," said Frank.

"I know." The young fellow sighed. "I called your home in Bayport. A Miss Hardy there told me about the cruise but begged me not to pester your father!"

"That's Aunt Gertrude." Joe chuckled.

"I rushed here to New York, thinking I might at least talk to him for an hour," the man went on. "You see, I've read in the newspapers of Mr. Hardy's great successes—"

The stranger paused, apparently suddenly recalling something.

"I've also read," he continued, "that his sons often help him out, and that they have solved some tough cases on their own. How about it? Would you all be willing to help me?"

"We'd like to. But," Joe replied doubtfully, "we've promised to go camping soon with a buddy."

"Let's hear your case, anyway," Frank suggested eagerly. "Maybe we can take it, Mr.—"

"I'm Bart Worth," the man said, his face showing relief. He looked about him.

"Is there a place near here where we can eat and talk?" he asked. "I was in such a hurry to catch your dad before he sailed I didn't have time for my supper."

"Sure. We'll listen while you eat," Joe said.

The Hardys led Mr. Worth up a side street. They stopped at a wide, steamy window bearing the lettering:

CHARLIE'S CLAM HOUSE

"I hear the food's good," Joe remarked, and the trio entered the restaurant.

It was a typical waterfront eating place, with sawdust on the floor. The place was crowded with diners, despite the late hour. In one corner sat a group of well-dressed people who, like the Hardys, had just left a farewell party on board the liner. But most of the customers were rough-looking men of the waterfront district. The noise of lively conversations and the odor of frying fish filled the air.

Frank, Joe, and Bart Worth seated themselves at a plain wooden table in the middle of the room. As soon as the waiter had taken a dinner order for Mr. Worth and sandwiches for the Hardys, the Southerner began his story.

"I'm owner, publisher, and editor of the *Larchmont Record*. You all probably never heard of us, but it's the only newspaper in the town of Larchmont, Georgia, on the Atlantic coast. Pretty soon there won't be any *Record,* though, if a certain man named Samuel Blackstone has his way!"

"How so?" Joe queried, as he and Frank leaned forward, deeply interested.

"Mr. Blackstone's suing me for libel," Worth

answered. "He's about the wealthiest business-man in Larchmont—the leading citizen."

"So his influence is considerable?" Frank prompted.

"You might say he about runs the town," admitted Bart Worth. "Besides, he's trying to ruin me and my newspaper."

"Why? Does Mr. Blackstone have a grudge against you?" Joe asked.

"I'll tell you more about Blackstone first," said the editor. "He lives on a large estate which is only half the original Blackstone property. Professor Ruel Rand, another Blackstone descendant, lives on the other half in the old family mansion. Clement Blackstone, the great-grandfather of both men, started the whole trouble. In his will, he divided the plantation between his son Benjamin and his daughter Blanche, who married a Rand. The difficulty began with the boundary line he set up."

Using a paper napkin, Bart Worth made a quick sketch.

"The only landmark mentioned in the will to indicate the property line was 'the great oak beside the big pond,'" the newspaperman pointed out. "Unfortunately there were *two* great oaks—one on either side of the pond."

"So both heirs claimed the pond!" Joe deduced.

"You've hit it exactly. The heirs bickered and feuded and went to court for years, but nothing was ever settled. Finally, in the time of Samuel Blackstone's grandfather, they gave up the dispute. Nobody in the family was interested in the pond any more. The Blackstones went into business and made money, and the Rands—well, they've been going downhill financially ever since. The old plantation house is pretty run-down now, although I guess Professor Rand doesn't mind it, being a bachelor."

"What about the libel suit, Mr. Worth?" Frank asked, intrigued.

"Well, a few weeks ago, I heard a rumor that Professor Rand had become interested in the disputed property all of a sudden, and that the old feud was on again!"

"You couldn't print a rumor, of course," Frank observed.

"No," the editor agreed, "but I went to the courthouse, where I learned that Rand *had* come in to examine old Clement's will. Then Jenny Shringle came to see me. Jenny's a seamstress, who worked many years for the Blackstones. Samuel's wife, who had been very fond of her, died about two years ago. Recently Jenny was discharged. Just before that, she told me she had personally overheard a quarrel between Blackstone and Professor Rand over the pond. Well, I acted very cautiously. I simply wrote a story that there *was* a rumor circulating—nothing more. That was a true fact, you see."

"And it's not libelous," Frank commented. "So you shouldn't have any problem there."

"That's not all," said the editor with increasing agitation. "When the story appeared in the *Record* it mentioned *another* rumor—a rumor that the Blackstone family fortune had been built on smuggling, and receiving stolen goods from pirates!"

"You didn't put that in?" Frank asked quickly.

"I certainly didn't!" Bart Worth exclaimed. "I wrote the original story myself. Everyone on my staff denies changing it. This pirate rumor *has* been common talk around Larchmont for years. Now that it's been printed in my paper, though, Blackstone is suing. He's touchy and proud—vain of his family's position. My only chance is to prove that the pirate rumor *is* true, which I honestly believe it is. If you fellows can't help me do that, I'll lose my newspaper!"

"Why not just apologize?" Frank asked. "Can't you explain things to Mr. Blackstone?"

The editor shook his head. "No. I've opposed his views and policies in the past in my paper, which has infuriated him. Now he has a motive for destroying it. Besides"—here the young man looked up with fire in his eyes—"Samuel Blackstone has called me a liar. I don't take that from anyone without a fight! And if he succeeds in ruining the *Record,* he'll have Larchmont completely bullied."

Just then the waiter arrived with the food. While the editor went to wash his hands, Joe sounded his brother out:

"What do you think? Shall we take the case?"

"I don't like it," Frank answered thoughtfully. "After all, this apparent libel was printed in Worth's paper. His claim that he doesn't know how it got there seems pretty weak. An editor *should* know what comes off his press."

"You don't trust him?"

"I think we should know more about this business before we commit ourselves, that's all," Frank declared.

Suddenly a huge hand and burly forearm stretched across the Hardys' table. "How about the ketchup?" demanded a rasping voice from the next table just behind Joe.

For the second time that night the boys heard heavy, wheezing breathing. They looked up and saw that the hand belonged to the husky man they had noticed near the gangplank.

"Sure. Help yourself," Joe said.

The stranger grunted and took the bottle.

A few moments later the young editor returned, and the three began to eat. Later, as they left the restaurant, Worth asked, "Well, will you take my case?"

He and the boys stood together on the sidewalk in front of the lighted window. A few customers, including the powerfully built man, came out the

"Someone in there is hurt!" Frank exclaimed

door and then disappeared down the dark street.

"We'll have to think about it, Mr. Worth," Frank answered, "and let you know."

Immediately the Southerner's face registered his disappointment. "I'm sorry," he said a little stiffly. "I had hoped at least that Mr. Hardy would give me some advice. Since I couldn't reach him, I thought you'd help me. However, here is my New York address." He wrote it on a piece of paper from a pocket notebook.

Then he said good night and walked away briskly. The Hardys started off in the opposite direction.

Huge warehouses lined the street on both sides. A single street light burned dimly on a distant corner. Suddenly, as the brothers came abreast of a dark doorway, a hoarse groan from inside reached their ears.

"Someone in there is hurt!" Frank exclaimed.

The boys stepped cautiously into the building. No sooner had they entered than the door slammed abruptly behind them. Four strong arms seized the Hardys, and rough palms were clapped over their mouths. The boys heard heavy, wheezy breathing.

"I'll teach you to mind your own business!" a threatening voice rasped.

Then came two quick, hard blows. Frank and Joe had been struck on the head. They slumped, unconscious, to the floor!

CHAPTER II

A Vanishing Victim

JOE was first to revive in the pitch-black warehouse. He listened tensely for the wheezy breathing of one of their attackers. Hearing nothing, Joe groped for his brother and shook him slightly.

"Joe . . . you all right?" Frank stammered, still groggy.

"Sure. We were decoyed in here by that groan and then knocked out. Remember?"

"Of all the greenhorns!" Frank murmured in disgust. "Caught by a trick like that!"

Joe rubbed his head gingerly. "At least it didn't leave a lump," he reported. "The fellows were experts. And did you hear that rasping breathing? Sounded like the tough guy we saw at the pier and in the clam house. He must have overheard Bart Worth talking to us, and tried to scare us off the case. But why?"

"Don't know. He picked the best way there is to encourage us," Frank retorted grimly. "We'll make that gorilla and his pal sorry they ever tangled with the Hardy brothers!"

This was no empty threat. Since solving their first mystery, *The Tower Treasure,* the brothers had built up a solid reputation as detectives by their shrewd sleuthing and resourcefulness in the face of danger. A recent case, *The Mark on the Door,* was their thirteenth successful adventure.

The boys picked themselves up, and made their way from the warehouse into the street. Luckily, an all-night cruising taxicab came by in a few minutes, and took them to their hotel.

Ten o'clock the next morning found Frank at the room telephone. "We've decided to accept your case, Mr. Worth," he told the editor. "We'll start by car for Larchmont early tomorrow, and probably arrive in two days."

"Fine! And thanks. I'm flying back tomorrow. Come to my office when you get there."

Next, Frank called the telegraph office and dictated a cable to Fenton Hardy in Jamaica:

STARTING NEW CASE TOMORROW
FOR MR. BART WORTH, LARCH-
MONT, GEORGIA

Joe now took over the phone and dialed the Bayport number of their plump, good-natured friend, Chet Morton. His cheerful voice answered. "Ready to go camping, now that your mother and dad have left?" he asked.

"Sure thing, Chet," Joe replied heartily. "Only, instead of Maine, we're going to the coast of Georgia. How's that sound?"

Several seconds of silence followed. Then came a suspicious query, "How come the switch?"

"A little business matter turned up."

"Business matter!" exploded Chet. "You don't fool me. Another mystery is what you mean. Another crazy, dangerous wild-goose chase that you're trying to drag poor ole Chet into!"

Chet Morton always insisted he hated danger, though he had shared most of the Hardy boys' hair-raising adventures.

"Then we can count you out?" asked Joe with a smile.

"Well . . ." came the grudging answer. "I've never been to Georgia. I could lie on the beach and leave you two to your narrow escapes."

"We'll pick you up at dawn tomorrow."

After a late breakfast in the hotel cafeteria, Frank and Joe, eager to start their sleuthing, took a train to Bayport. As soon as they reached home, the boys kissed their tall, angular aunt, then told her the plans. Aunt Gertrude, at times sharp-tongued and peppery despite her pride in her nephews, gave her opinion of the whole expedition.

"Foolishness," she declared. "It'll end in

trouble, you mark me. And then Fenton will have to rush away from the Caribbean to help you. My poor brother!"

"Oh, Auntie! You know Dad wouldn't want us to turn down a challenging case!" Joe said.

"Humph! I guess not. Well, you'd better have a good meal, anyway. And maybe you'd like to invite Chet."

This was done, and it was decided that Chet and his gear would spend the night at the Hardys' because of the early start. Then Frank backed the boys' powerful yellow convertible into the driveway. He and Joe packed sleeping bags, tents, cooking equipment, spare clothing, and the Hardys' skin-diving equipment into it.

Aunt Gertrude prepared one of her delicious dinners. Chet, as usual, had second helpings of everything.

"You'd better know," Miss Hardy told them later, "that there was a big, tough-looking man hanging around here this afternoon before you boys returned. He even came up our driveway. I called out to see what he wanted. Apparently that scared him away."

"For good, I hope," Frank said. The same thought occurred to him and Joe. Had their hoarse-voiced attacker preceded them to Bayport? The boys changed the subject, however, not wanting to worry Aunt Gertrude unnecessarily.

Just at dawn the next morning, after break-

fast and good-bys to Miss Hardy, the yellow convertible, with Frank, Chet, and Joe in the front
seat, purred through the quiet Bayport streets.
Soon it entered the superhighway heading north.

"Now," said Frank, who was driving, "if anybody's watching us, he'll think we're still going
to Maine!"

"I wish we were," declared Chet. The brothers
had given him the details of their new case.

About ten miles farther, however, Frank sent
the car down an exit ramp, passed underneath
the thruway, and entered the highway on the
other side. Now they were bound for Georgia!

The remainder of that day, and the next, they
sped along the smooth concrete under a warm sun
and blue sky. About noon on the last day of the
boys' journey, a cluster of police cars, with red
lights winking, warned of an accident ahead.
Passing by slowly, the brothers and Chet saw a
yellow convertible, the same model as the Hardys', turned upside down on the center grass strip.

"Gives me the creeps!" Chet shuddered. "It
might have been us!"

When Frank reached the next service area, he
pulled in to have lunch at the counter. The boys
had just finished eating when two state troopers
came in and took seats nearby.

"A bad smashup," said the first officer. "The
driver and passenger thrown clear, lucky for them.
It was deliberate, too. A blue sedan forced them

right off the road. The driver of the car behind them saw the whole thing, but didn't catch a glimpse of the license number."

"Can't our boys stop the sedan farther along?" asked the other trooper.

"No. It must have turned off at the next exit. The witness caught a glimpse of the driver, though. Big, flat-faced fellow. Had a blond-haired man with him."

Frank, Joe, and Chet paid their check and filed out quietly. They climbed into the convertible with serious faces.

"That 'accident' was meant for us!" declared Joe as they started once again. "The driver sounds like our suspicious friend with the wheezy breathing."

Constantly alert, the young detectives continued their journey. Joe, now at the wheel, turned off the highway and continued south on the secondary road, to throw off pursuit.

Late that afternoon they rolled into Larchmont, an old town built around a main square containing the courthouse and a Civil War monument. Stores lined the edges of the square, and the boys soon spotted the building which housed the *Record's* offices, which were on the second floor. While Frank and Chet waited in the car, Joe ran inside and came back with a smiling Bart Worth.

"Glad to see you!" said the young editor. He was introduced to Chet and shook hands with him. "Joe says you all want to camp. I'll take you out now and show you the best spot."

He directed Frank to follow the same road by which the boys had entered town. About a mile out of town, he said, "Turn right on this lane. It leads to the beach about a mile away. Only fishermen use the lane."

Bart Worth explained that half a mile farther along the main road was the entrance to the Blackstone home. "It's about halfway between the shore and the public road. Professor Rand has his own driveway some distance from Blackstone's."

The lane made its way among scrubby pine trees. Finally the car came to the beach where the fishermen's road, barely discernible, turned left.

"Boy, that ocean smells good!" Chet declared.

Presently Bart Worth said, "This road ends at the dunes ahead. They spread along the shore and I figured it would be an ideal spot for you all to camp out. Nobody will know you're around."

The boys selected a secluded spot between two high dunes, then quickly pitched their camp. Leaving Chet to unpack provisions, Frank and Joe drove the editor back to town.

A tall, pale man with blond hair, wearing a linen suit and straw hat, stopped them as they entered the newspaper office.

"Hello there, Mr. Worth," he said. "I see you have company."

"Yes, a couple of visitors from up North," Worth responded. "Boys, this is Mr. Henry Cutter—a Yankee like yourselves. Mr. Cutter and his partner, Mr. Stewart, are in the antique business. They're down here looking over business opportunities."

"That's right," agreed Cutter, appraising the Hardys with hard blue eyes. "Once in a while we put an ad in the *Record* for people interested in helping us start a profitable business. We make trips into the countryside around Larchmont."

After shaking hands, the Hardys followed Worth into his private office. Here they discussed the Blackstone case and how the young sleuths would first tackle it.

"We'll take a little tour of the grounds tonight," Frank decided.

"Okay," Bart said. "Keep me posted."

When the brothers were driving back on the lane, Joe asked, "What did you think of Mr. Cutter?"

"Seemed to me we got a good once-over from Cutter for just a casual meeting," Frank commented.

Back at camp, Chet and the Hardys took a swim. Then, using their camp stove, they prepared a tasty meal of hash and brown bread. After eating, and burying the debris, the three sat and talked in low tones until dusk came on. The continually moving sea had darkened, as the sunset's afterglow gave way to stars. The air grew close and murky.

"I think it's time to inspect the Blackstone property," Frank proposed. "It's dark enough now."

"You two go," Chet suggested quickly. "I'll stay and guard camp."

A few minutes later the brothers set off on foot among the dunes toward the Blackstone house. It was difficult walking through the high grass and loose sand. Here and there a lone scraggly pine endeavored to exist.

Presently the earth became less sandy. The scraggly pines gave way to thick vegetation, more and more tangled.

"According to Bart's directions, we ought to come to the pond soon," muttered Joe, beaming his flashlight ahead.

The thick, forbidding tangle made hard going, even with flashlights. At last the brothers struck a path through clumps of swamp grass, matted vines, and huge rotting trees. Then an open space appeared ahead. Their lights shone on an expanse of still, brackish-looking water.

"Blackstone's place should be to the right," said Frank, plunging forward in a northerly direction.

Some distance beyond, the brothers discerned house lights ahead. There was a narrow path which they followed through swampy ground. An ominous growling reached their ears, and they skirted a pen containing two big, fierce-looking dogs.

"Look, Joe!" Frank exclaimed, pointing to the large, imposing white-pillared mansion before them.

The boys stopped and stared at a brightly lighted, partially open window. Through it they saw three men. One, facing them, was large and portly. The other was tall, dark, and gangling. A Negro servant, wearing a white butler's coat, stood near the door.

As the Hardys approached stealthily, the men's voices reached them.

"Rand, you'll get it over my dead body!" shouted the heavy-set man.

"The big one's Blackstone, no doubt," Joe whispered. "Wonder what Rand is after."

The tall man, obviously furious, said something indistinguishable. Suddenly Blackstone, his face livid, seized a heavy china vase from a desk and smashed it against the professor's head!

Instantly the light went out. Frank and Joe dashed up the steps and pounded on the door. Within twenty-five seconds it was opened.

"Yes?"

The Negro servant who had been in the room stood looking at the boys calmly from the hallway.

"We'd like to see Mr. Blackstone—right away!" Frank cried.

Without a word, the servant ushered the brothers into the bay-windowed room. There, comfortably seated in an easy chair and reading a book, was the large man. To the Hardys' profound astonishment, they found no trace of Professor Rand.

Even more astonishing was the fact that the china vase which had been smashed against his head stood whole upon the desk!

CHAPTER III

Water Monster

FOR A moment Frank and Joe remained too astonished to speak. The heavy-set man put down his book and stood up.

"You want to see me?" he asked gruffly.

"Yes. You *are* Mr. Blackstone?" Frank spoke up.

"I am. What do you want?"

"We . . . we heard a cry, and thought maybe there had been an accident!"

"Accident?" The man gave the brothers a steely look of suspicion. "No, there's been no accident that I know of. I've been spending a quiet evening reading. You're the first visitors I've had tonight. By the way, what are *you* doing on my property?"

"We're visiting the area," Joe answered promptly. "We've just been exploring the beach and came up here."

"Treacherous swamp around here," Mr. Blackstone commented. "Incidentally, my dogs are usually let loose at night, so I wouldn't advise your getting lost in this direction again. Minnie! Show these young men to the door."

A young Negro maid entered the room. The Hardys were surprised. They had expected to see the somewhat elderly man who had answered their knock. They looked around for him on the way out. But he, too, was gone.

"If we hadn't *both* seen that fight I'd think I was crazy," Joe muttered, as he and Frank left.

"Oh—oh," Frank whispered. "Mr. Blackstone has another caller." A linen-suited figure was approaching on foot up the drive.

"Mr. Cutter!" Joe exclaimed.

A moment later tall Henry Cutter mounted the steps. He glanced at the boys sharply, but merely nodded as he went past them into the house.

"Wonder what *he's* here for," Frank mused.

For a few minutes the brothers lingered under a huge spreading cypress near the house. They saw Blackstone draw the curtains across the bay window, but still his gruff voice could be heard clearly.

"Those boys? Just a couple of nosy Northerners. I got rid of them. Look here, Cutter, it's no use coming around. I won't sell."

The men apparently moved away from the window, for the young detectives could hear no more.

As quickly as possible they retraced their steps to the pond, and toward camp.

"What happened to Professor Rand?" asked Joe. "I thought he got a knockout wallop. And how did Blackstone mend that broken vase so fast?"

"I couldn't even see a crack in it," Frank added.

"I wonder what Cutter wants to buy from Blackstone," Joe said. "Something for his antique business?"

"Wish I had an answer," his brother replied wryly. "Let's try our luck at Rand's home tomorrow."

As they ate an early breakfast, Chet pointed out a dilapidated fishing smack some distance off shore. "Wonder what's running," he murmured.

Frank and Joe did not reply. They set off for the pond. Reaching it, they turned left.

"We'll get Rand's story about last night," Frank declared.

Huge live oaks, hung with Spanish moss, partly hid a stately white Southern mansion in need of paint. Wisteria blossoms hung bell-like from vines climbing the walls. The Hardys mounted the steps of the still stately portico, supported by high, once-white round columns.

Frank knocked repeatedly on the door. There was no response. As they circled the neglected structure, they rapped on windows, called out, pounded on side and back doors, with no results.

"The professor's not here—or he just doesn't want visitors," Joe concluded. "All right, then—back to Blackstone's!"

Samuel Blackstone's estate, with its carefully tended flower beds and pruned shrubbery made a sharp contrast with his cousin's run-down property. When Frank spotted a young gardener pushing a power mower, he strolled over to him.

"Lookin' for somebody?" The pleasant-faced young man squinted at them in the bright sunshine.

"Yes—the elderly butler who works for Mr. Blackstone," Joe answered. "We can't find him."

"Grover?" the gardener drawled. "Well, now, he's gone on vacation—just this morning, I hear. First one in thirty-five years. Don't it beat all?"

"Sure does." Joe laughed. But the minute he and Frank were alone, Frank noted, "Mighty sudden vacation, if you ask me."

"Very," Joe agreed tersely as he followed the drive, which looped around the house before leading to the road. The route took them past the dog pen. The police dogs leaped and whined as though eager to attack the boys.

"I'd sure hate to have them at my throat!" Joe remarked, grinning.

Meanwhile, Frank had been thinking out the boys' next step. "We'd better head for Larchmont," he advised, "and look up Jenny Shringle. She overheard Rand and Blackstone quarreling before, and according to Bart, she also told him the rumor that the Blackstone money originally came from smuggling."

"Why did she tell Worth all this?" Joe wondered, as he and Frank hurried toward their camp.

"Revenge," Frank reasoned. "She'd been a seamstress in the family for years, and just lately Blackstone fired her. She probably wanted to get square with him."

The brothers brought Chet up to date on the news, then set off in the convertible for Larchmont. Frank consulted a slip of paper, then watched the street signs until he found the one he wanted. He turned onto an unpaved road that ended in a steep railway embankment. The houses along the road were small and dingy.

"Here we are," Frank announced, pointing to a boxlike cottage overgrown by scraggly bushes. The Hardys went to the door and knocked.

"Meow!" A black-and-white cat came around the corner and rubbed herself against the boys' legs. Once more Frank rapped urgently.

"Meow," was the only answer.

"Here, kitty, kitty, kitty!" sang a voice nearby.

Turning, the Hardys saw a heavy, middle-aged woman calling from the porch of the house next door. In her hands she held a saucer of milk.

"Miss Shringle?" Frank inquired.

"No. And I don't know where Jenny is," replied the woman, who appeared willing and even eager to talk. "But it's right strange about her going. She left here without providing for her cat."

After placing the saucer on the ground, the neighbor continued, "Now this is why it's funny. She left the house yesterday morning *just after dawn*. That's not a time for law-abidin' folks to be about. Jenny had no suitcase, and not even a pocketbook. Just slipped out in her best dress— really a little old shabby black one—and an old flowered hat."

"Do you know where she went?" Joe asked.

The woman shrugged. "I reckon she walked out to the main road. Maybe somebody sent for her. Maybe not. But why be so sneaky about it?"

The Hardys were noncommittal in order not to arouse the woman's suspicions. Soon the brothers said good-by and returned to camp for lunch.

After eating, and telling Chet about the strange disappearance, the chums rested under some pines near the tent.

"Three people involved in this case have disappeared," Joe summed up in exasperation.

"And no leads as to where they might have gone!" Frank added.

Chet yawned. "Maybe we should report these disappearances to Mr. Worth or the police."

"Let's wait one more day," Frank urged. "I want to explore the pond tonight. After all, it's the central issue in this whole case. If we don't turn up anything, we'll call in the authorities."

"Well, I'll hold the fort here," Chet offered cheerfully. "Fishing's great."

That evening, the hazy light of dusk found the two detectives advancing quietly among the sand dunes and the tall grass. Because of the insects, they had smeared their arms and faces with repellent. Also, as a precaution against an onslaught by Blackstone's dogs, Joe carried a stout club.

In the dim light the dead trees and hummocks of swamp grass assumed fantastic shapes. Frogs croaked, and now and then one would slip with a gurgle into a brown, stagnant pool. At last the boys reached the pond between the two properties.

"This way," whispered Frank, turning left. "Let's try Rand's side first."

He and Joe pushed through the dense growth around the pond's edge. It was totally dark when they emerged at a flat, open space. Before them rose the branchless trunk of an ancient oak tree, nearly twenty feet high. It was silhouetted against a moonlit but partly clouded sky.

Carefully the boys examined the remains of the old tree. "This must be one of the trees mentioned in the will," Frank said, as the boys made their way back along the pond until they came to the Blackstone side of the water. Here the oak stump was shorter.

Disappointed, Frank and Joe switched off their lights and looked around. Overhead, moonlight glowed silver around the fringe of a cloud. Suddenly Joe grasped Frank's arm and whispered, "Over there!" The yellow beam of a flashlight could be plainly seen on the far rim of the pond.

The light moved around the oak stump like some giant firefly. Once, when the moon sailed free of clouds, the boys caught a glimpse of a tall, dark figure, pacing back and forth.

"He's looking for something!" Frank whispered.

"Suppose it's Rand?"

The light began moving around the edge of the pond toward them. Nearer and nearer it came. The boys waited breathlessly. But before they could make a move, heavy, crashing steps retreated through the underbrush and died away.

"We should've nabbed him!" Joe said in disgust.

"At this distance?" Frank said. Then he pointed in amazement toward the middle of the pond.

The white moon, thinly veiled by a few mackerel clouds, showed up a sudden roiling disturbance on the glassy surface. Large circles of rippling water were expanding outward. At their center a gleaming row of finlike humps slid into view. A fantastic, monstrous head rose briefly, dripping, into the moonlight. Then it sank beneath the dark waters!

CHAPTER IV

Skin-Diving Sleuths

THE Hardy boys could almost believe they had beheld a prehistoric creature with its jagged fin and enormous head. Frank and Joe peered in fascination at the swamp-bordered pond.

"There it is again!" Joe whispered in awe.

The grotesque shape had again surfaced, and now cut through the water to the rear bank. Here it wriggled up and disappeared.

"Come on!" Joe cried, switching on his flashlight. "Let's go after that thing!"

They found the swamp at the rear of the pond almost impassable. Stumbling over roots, dodging under hanging moss, sinking in the rank mire, the two boys doggedly made their way along.

"That monster must have come out near here!" Frank panted, shining his light around.

In this spot the thick vegetation grew right to the water's edge. The Hardys plunged through the tangle until they felt the tepid water lap over their sneakers.

Their flashlight beams picked out crushed leaves and stalks where something large must have dragged itself ashore. But the trail ended a few feet from the water, in the thick growth. No further signs of the strange creature could be found.

"Maybe the monster slipped back into the pond," Joe whispered apprehensively.

Suddenly Frank snapped off his flashlight and signaled his brother to do the same. At the edge of the gloomy pond, where the big swamp stretched toward the main road, a light was moving!

In a moment the Hardys were fighting their way through the dense undergrowth toward the figure. The moon was their only light, as they crept forward silently and swiftly. Soon a glow about fifty yards ahead of them lit up a grove of weird, moss-covered cypress trees. Underneath one of them, Frank and Joe discerned a tall figure in a long coat and floppy hat, his back to the boys.

Scarcely breathing, Frank and Joe slipped forward. In one hand the strange figure carried a small lantern. He frequently stooped to examine the ground. Once he crouched for a long time looking at something. The boys crept closer.

Suddenly the figure stood to his full height, as if listening keenly. Then, like a shot, he went off at a swift, long-legged run through the swamp.

"He's heading for Rand's!" Frank whispered tensely, as the boys raced forward.

A protruding root suddenly sent Joe sprawling. Frank, behind, piled on top of him. Ahead, the figure with the swinging lantern gained ground. Leaping to their feet, the boys ran on, out of the swamp and up a slight hill toward the Rand estate. Presently, a high, solid hedge, silhouetted against the moonlit sky, came into view. At the same moment, the pursued man and his lantern disappeared into the dense shrubbery. Panting, the boys pounded up and plunged through it.

"Whoa!" cried Frank.

Beyond the hedge the ground dropped off sharply about seven feet. Below them lay a broad meadow. The man with the lantern was not in sight.

"Given us the slip," Joe admitted.

Still breathing hard from the chase, the brothers walked directly toward the ocean. They found Chet at camp, lying on his stomach, munching an apple and reading a mystery story.

"Hi! Good night! Where have you been? Swimming in mud?" he needled, looking at their soggy, spattered clothing.

Joe grinned. "Chet, you must go up to the pond and see the monster!"

"The—what? No, thanks. But you're kidding?"

"We mean it," Frank replied, and he told the story, exaggerating it a bit to tease Chet. "You're really missing all the excitement, Chet."

"It's okay with me. I'll pull a fish out of the water—that'll be monster enough for me."

He arose, lighted the camp stove, and prepared mugs of steaming cocoa. Suddenly he said, "Wait a minute, fellows! Did you really see some kind of prehistoric . . . dinosaur . . . in that pond?"

"Well, not quite that big." Frank had to laugh. "But the thing was as big as a man, at least."

Chet looked around fearfully. "Do you think the monster might be connected with the mystery?"

"Search me," Joe shrugged. "I wonder if that prowler out there tonight saw the creature."

"Funny business." Chet shook his head.

The campers finished their cocoa, then crawled into their bags and slept soundly. After breakfast next morning, the boys attended Sunday church service. They had lunch in town, then Frank said, "Let's drive to Professor Rand's house. If the professor isn't there, we'll go to the police. I don't care what Blackstone says. We *saw* Rand take a nasty crack on the head. He may be seriously injured, or worse!"

When the three boys reached the run-down plantation house, they found it as empty as it had appeared the day before. They headed at full speed for Larchmont and went to Bart Worth's home.

"You have news?" he asked expectantly.

Joe related the fierce quarrel the Hardys had witnessed in the Blackstone mansion two nights before. "Bart," the boy went on, "has anyone mentioned having seen the professor lately?"

The young editor shook his head and grabbed his hat in one movement. "It's a case for the police now," he said, rising. But Frank restrained him.

"You'd better not become involved," the boy advised. "After all, Joe and I were the witnesses. The police know you have a feud with Blackstone, and might not believe you. Also, we don't want Blackstone to know we're working for you."

Bart agreed, and the boys left to make a report to the authorities.

Larchmont's police station was a trim building of whitewashed brick, just across the square from the courthouse. A desk sergeant led the three into the office of Police Chief Gerald. Frank gave an account of the attack to the middle-aged law officer, who listened intently.

"Hmm . . . by the time you entered the room, the vase had been mended," the chief repeated. He stared ahead in deep thought. "What do you young fellows want me to do?" he asked.

"We think you should procure a warrant and search Blackstone's house," Frank urged promptly.

The chief smiled, picked up the telephone, and dialed a number.

"Hello?" he began politely. "Mr. Blackstone, this is Chief Gerald. Some visitors to our town have been telling me about a fight at your place two nights ago. One of the men—Professor Rand, by the sound of it—is supposedly missing. I'm afraid I'll be obliged to get a warrant and make a search of your place."

The three boys watched the officer's face eagerly for some hint of Blackstone's reaction. But they could tell nothing until the chief hung up. He looked at the boys quizzically and reported, "Mr. Blackstone says I don't need a warrant. Told me to come on out there right now, and bring the visitors with me—that he hasn't anything to hide."

Chief Gerald summoned one of his patrolmen and led Frank, Joe, and Chet to a police car outside. Within twenty minutes they were parked in front of the large brick house. Samuel Blackstone stood waiting on the porch.

"This way, Chief," he greeted the law officer, not waiting for an introduction to Chet Morton. "I want you to see everything." The heavy-set man did not address the boys directly.

Mr. Blackstone conducted them to every part of his house. Frank and Joe kept a sharp watch, but saw nothing out of the ordinary. Finally, he led the group to the front door.

"You've seen the house," said Blackstone. "Now read this."

He produced a note written on Professor Rand's stationery. The chief read it aloud:

" 'Dear Samuel, if you want me I'm at the Storm Island Lighthouse for a few days, doing some research. Ruel.' "

"My cousin is an archaeologist," Blackstone explained. "His specialty is American Indian civilization. He's always looking for old relics."

"Well, this note sounds friendly enough," commented Gerald as he handed it back.

"And are *you* satisfied?" The big man suddenly turned hard, antagonistic eyes on the Hardys.

"Not yet," Joe spoke up without flinching. "We'd like to talk to your man, Grover. He saw that fight, too."

"Grover's older brother in Chicago is very ill," Blackstone returned promptly. "He begged me to let him go to see him, and I did. It's his first vacation in many years, and I won't have him brought back for any such nonsensical reason."

Blackstone accompanied the boys and the police officer when they returned to the waiting patrol car. "Chief Gerald," he said warningly, "these boys have already trespassed on my land. Now they practically accuse me of something underhanded. If they ever set foot on my property again, or annoy me in any way, I'm going to ask you to arrest them!"

Turning quickly, he strode back to the house. Then the police car drove out of the long private road and back toward Larchmont.

"Well, boys," the chief told them, "you've made a powerful enemy."

"That doesn't bother us," Frank said. "Not if we find out the truth."

That afternoon, back at their camp, the three young detectives held a conference. "We must find out why that pond is so important," Frank insisted. "I'm for going back there tonight with our skin-diving gear, and tracking down the monster!"

That evening, as a big, round yellow moon rose above the trees of the dark swamp, the three boys stood at the pond's edge. Frank and Joe, in bathing trunks, held diving face masks and flippers. Each had an aqualung strapped to his back. Chet stood by with a Thermos of hot broth.

"Well, here goes," said Frank quietly. He put on his mask, adjusted his breathing hose, and slipped into the black water.

The next instant Chet and Joe were startled by a sudden crash of brush on the far side of the pond. As the boys stared almost hypnotized, a huge shape making remarkably little noise wriggled off the bank into the water.

Seconds later, a saw-tooth fin broke the smooth moonlit surface of the pond and headed straight for the spot where Frank had gone under!

CHAPTER V

Marooned!

"THE monster! It's after Frank!" cried Joe as the creature's long serrate fin disappeared beneath the pond's surface.

Quickly adjusting his own face mask and breathing tube, Joe plunged into the dark, menacing water. He kicked powerfully with his flippers, and shot down through the water. The bottom of the pond was absolutely black, but just enough of the moon's pale light filtered down through the murk for him to distinguish violent thrashing motions dead ahead.

Instantly Joe encircled his brother's shoulder with one arm. At the same time, he came to grips with something cold and slippery that was tugging Frank's limp body deeper into the pond.

Fearlessly Joe attacked. But the creature possessed great power and gradually wrestled him down into the thick ooze at the bottom.

Frank and Chet sat on the wooden box housing the engine. Soon the craft was moving toward the mouth of the inlet into the Atlantic.

"Storm Island is a little south of here," explained Frank, opening a chart. "It's nothing but a pile of rocks in the sea, according to Worth. The light hasn't been used in years, since there's no more shipping from Larchmont."

They left the harbor and headed the boat south on the blue-green sea. The white dunes of the beach were far over to their right. The horizon was a line where the powder-blue sky met the darker hue of the ocean. Then a pile of jumbled rocks came into view.

"Must be Storm Island," Frank said briefly.

As they came closer, they saw that the islet was indeed nothing but a mass of rock, about a hundred yards long. From its center rose a conical wooden tower with a black roof and gaping windows.

They landed at a little stone jetty. and tied up the boat, then mounted some stone steps that apparently led to a path to the lighthouse. Quickly the boys looked around for the gangling figure of the professor. No one was in sight.

"Professor Rand!" Joe called out. No answer.

The boys walked around the islet, peering into crevices of jagged rocks, and calling out periodically. There was no response.

"Maybe he's inside the lighthouse," Chet said.

The young sleuths entered the deserted rooms at the bottom of the now run-down tower, where lighthouse keepers had made their home in years past. Finding nothing, they climbed the winding enclosed staircase. At one point two steps were missing and the three friends had to reach up to the third one above.

At the top of the lighthouse was a round platform with the large, old-fashioned light in the center of it. Several of the broad glass windowpanes had been broken.

Suddenly Joe cried out. "Hey! Our boat!"

He pointed down to the landward side of the islet. Drifting rapidly away from the jetty was their rented craft! In the distance, a pleasure speedboat plowed away from the island.

Turning, Frank and Joe clattered down the old

wooden steps. Chet followed close behind. "Our food's aboard!" he groaned.

The trio emerged from the lighthouse and dashed down to the jetty. By this time their boat

had already drifted a distance too great to swim.

"I'm sure I tied those lines tightly!" Frank declared. "They were cut—by somebody in that speedboat, I'll bet."

"But why?" Joe burst out. "Boy, what a mess! Not only have we come way out here on a wild-goose chase, but to top it off, we're marooned!"

Chet was so dejected at this thought he could only groan again, "All our food gone!" The boys returned to the lighthouse and took stock of their situation. From every point of view it seemed desperate.

"We have one quart of drinking water in my canteen," Chet informed them, "and one package of cookies I brought in my pocket. Oh, all that wonderful cheese, meat, and—I can't stand it!"

"No ocean-going vessels pass anywhere near here," Frank put in glumly. "And I guess this isn't a popular spot for pleasure cruising. The water's too rough!"

"The boat owner thinks *we're* on a pleasure ride," Joe added, "but he doesn't know where. And somehow I doubt that Cutter and his pal will advise anyone if *they* find out we're missing."

Frank jumped up. "Let's go outside and see if there's anything on this island we can rig for a signal!"

All afternoon the youths explored their sea-locked prison. The island was composed of sharp, craggy rock faces with steep drops in between.

The surf on the ocean side had made a network of shelving ledges and hollow caves.

At suppertime they sat down on the rocks and Chet doled out to each boy a ration of two chocolate cookies and two swallows of water. As they chewed their meager meal, staring idly at the old tower, Frank burst out:

"I know what! We always carry match packets with us when on a camping trip, so let's light the beacon tonight as a distress signal. All these old-fashioned lighthouses used acetylene beacons. If we can't make this one work, what good is the chemistry we're learning in high school?"

Eagerly Frank led the way into the lighthouse. Sure enough, in a small ground-floor room directly at the center of the tower, they found a big tank with a pipe rising up toward the light.

"But where will we get the gas for the tank?" Chet wanted to know.

At that moment Joe pried the lid off an old drum. "Here we are—calcium carbide!"

Frank explained. "We put some of this chemical in the tank and pour sea water over it. The chemical reaction produces acetylene gas, which burns with a bright white light."

Already dusk was falling. They sent Chet out with a bucket for sea water. Meanwhile, Joe climbed the staircase to the beacon. There he found a big metal ring with multiple jets. Looking out one of the broad, paneless windows, he saw Chet returning with his bucket of water.

Then Joe heard the tinkering of metal far below. He took a packet of matches from his pocket and held one ready to strike.

"Okay!" came the muffled signal. "Light her!"

Crouching, Joe held his flaring match to the jets. The stiff breeze, whipping through the wide window, snuffed it out. Again and again he brought a flame over the holes, but without result. Finally, all his matches were gone. At that moment the boy heard the floor creak nearby.

As Joe turned, something lifted him up and rushed him toward the wide-open window. With a wild cry of "Help!" Joe felt himself plunging into space!

CHAPTER VI

Signal Fire

DEEP in the tower, Frank and Chet were electrified to hear a wild cry for help, and then another fainter call, which seemed to come from outside the lighthouse.

"Fra-ank!"

"It's Joe!" cried Frank. He sprinted up the rickety staircase so fast that the structure shook underneath him. Chet ran behind.

The two piled into the empty beacon room. For a moment Frank and Chet heard only the strong wind sweeping through and the sound of the sea breaking on the rocks below. Then came a kicking sound outside.

Frank rushed to the window. Two tanned hands clung to the sill. Over the side, in the early evening darkness, he could see Joe dangling ninety feet above the sharp rocks.

"Chet! Over here!" Frank yelled, at the same

time seizing his brother's wrists. The hefty boy was at his side in a second. Together, they hauled Joe in to safety.

"Somebody—threw me—out!" the boy gasped as he sank to the floor to rest. "I managed to grab the sill."

"Thank goodness you did," said Frank.

Chet said in astonishment, "But there's nobody on the island!"

"Wait!" Frank signaled abruptly. "Quiet!"

Speechless, the three boys listened. The sea crashed over the rocks. The wind hummed through the room. Did they also hear creaking on the old staircase below?

Frank hurried stealthily halfway down the steps. But he neither saw nor heard anything and returned to the platform.

"You sure the wind didn't blow you out?" Chet asked Joe. "It's pretty strong."

"No." By now Joe had recovered from his close call. "I was grabbed and pushed through the window. No doubt about it."

"But how could anybody have climbed the stairs without our knowing it?" Frank frowned.

"There's got to be an answer," Joe returned. "Let's have a look at the stairs. Anybody got a flashlight?"

Chet produced a tiny one from a pocket, but it would not light. "Guess it needs new batteries," he apologized.

Frank brought out a packet of matches and lighted their way down. When he reached the two missing steps, Frank cautiously leaned down into the open space and struck another match. A network of thick diagonal supporting beams was revealed in the flickering light.

"A risky place to hide," he said. "But it could be done by a strong and agile person."

"We'd better face up to it," Joe said somberly. "We're being dogged by a dangerous enemy, and he's on this island with us!"

"Yes," Frank agreed, swiftly piecing together recent events. "He must have been dropped off by that speedboat we saw heading away. Then he untied our boat and hid among the rocks until he heard us mention lighting the beacon."

"You mean he slipped up to the tower ahead of us?" Chet asked.

Frank nodded. "He stayed behind these supports until Joe climbed to the beacon, then followed. He slipped down the stairs while we were pulling Joe in. That was the creaking we heard."

"All right," agreed Joe. "But we'll have a hard time finding him at night if he's hiding out in those rocks. We have nothing but matches."

Frank and Chet pulled out their packets, which were only partly filled.

Most of these matches were used to hunt for the fourth person who, they learned, was not inside the lighthouse.

"Only one thing for us to do," said Frank. "We'll lock the door and bunk in the keeper's quarters. Whoever our enemy is can spend the night on the rocks! Then in the morning we'll find him."

"Good plan," Joe assented. "We'll take turns standing guard."

As Frank took the first watch, Joe and Chet stretched out on the floor to sleep. At midnight Frank awakened the stout boy. Joe took the early-morning shift. There had not been a disturbing sound during the night.

At dawn the three stranded sleuths emerged from the lighthouse. A red ball of sun was coming out of the steel-gray sea. A light mist hung over the water.

"The third straight meal I've missed," moaned Chet in a voice of genuine suffering.

Manfully, however, he handed round a breakfast of cookies and two gulps of water apiece. "Just enough for lunch and supper," he said, and carefully stored the provisions again. "Maybe I can catch a fish later."

"Now, let's find our enemy," said Frank. "And stay together, so we can handle him when we do!"

All morning, as the sun rose higher, the boys combed the deep cuts and passageways in the rocks.

"How could anybody hide here?" Chet wondered.

"He couldn't," Joe assured him. "I believe someone came back here in a boat and took the intruder away. Probably turned off the motor and used oars so we wouldn't hear what was going on."

Chet now asked, "Why didn't the beacon work last night?"

"Gas didn't get up to the light," Joe reported. "I never did smell it. Probably there's a break in the old line."

"How about the lamps up there?" suggested Chet. He referred to a circle of oil lamps, backed by once-shiny tin reflectors, extending all around the tower platform.

"No oil," Frank said. "Those go back to the days when this light was built—long before it was converted to acetylene."

At that moment Joe, in his dark-blue jersey, gazed at the tower. Frank looked at his brother, then at his own maroon shirt. Finally he stared with sudden hope at Chet's white garment, which blazed with a wild, colorful design.

"Say, what are you up to?" the chunky boy asked uneasily.

"We need your shirt," replied Joe. "It'll be a perfect distress flag."

With a martyred air, Chet pulled off his shirt, and the Hardys rigged it on the shaft of an old broom in the lighthouse. They mounted the signal on the tower.

"So far, so good," Joe said when they were on

the ground once more. "What about a signal for tonight? Let's find something to make a fire."

Another tour of the island turned up only a few sodden bits of driftwood. After a cheerless lunch of water and cookies, Frank and Joe went to scour the lighthouse for fuel, while Chet tried his best to snare a fish but failed.

After a time the brothers dragged out a heavy armchair with the stuffing about to burst from the seams. While they kicked this apart, Chet looked curiously at a little brick structure about the size of a dog kennel.

"Hello—an old brick oven," he thought.

The opening had been sealed up with brick and masonry. Chet worked at the mortar with his pocketknife. It crumbled, and Chet pulled out the bricks. He peered inside.

"A tin box!" he yelled. "Treasure!"

Instantly Frank and Joe left their demolished chair and rushed over.

"There's more than treasure," Joe said excitedly, peering in. "Look at that pile of newspapers! Now we'll get a fire going tonight!"

He yanked out a great stack of old papers, somewhat damp and moldy with age.

"What's new in the world?" quipped Chet. "Say, these are funny newspapers. No headlines."

" 'The relief of General McClellan from command of the American Federal armies has been announced,' " Joe read from one of the small-print columns. "Hey! It's all about the Civil War. These papers were published in London."

"Our history teacher will shoot us if we burn these," Chet objected.

"If we *don't* burn them, we may never see our history class again," Frank reminded him. "Let's just hope we won't have to. Open that tin box, Chet."

Using his knife, the stout boy complied. Inside was a package of papers, carefully tied with a printed note on top.

"It says these papers were saved from the *Sally Ann,* an English ship returning to America, when she was wrecked on the reef," he announced.

"Dull stuff, probably," commented Joe. With Chet's help, he began spreading the old newspapers in the sun to dry, weighting them with bricks from the oven.

Frank, meanwhile, leafed through the little package of documents. They were mostly shipping invoices and insurance papers for the ship's cargo. Dull stuff, as Joe had said. But then, tucked among them, a note on plain white paper caught his attention. Suddenly he leaped to his feet.

"Joe! Chet! Listen to this! It's a memo from the *Sally Ann's* captain to himself!"

When the other two had dashed over, astonished, Frank read the memo:

" 'Last voyage—my friend, Clement Blackstone, embarked with his entire family for England, from Hidden Harbor. Before sailing, Clement informed me, as his boyhood friend, that the family fortune and papers were hidden nearby, and gave me directions for finding them, in case he should never return. Memorized directions in order to avoid committing them to writing.' "

Joe gave a whistle. "Maybe you didn't find a treasure, Chet, but you've given us a clue to one. But where's Hidden Harbor? There's nothing hidden about Larchmont's inlet."

"Hidden Harbor," Frank mused. "Wherever it is, the Blackstone fortune is nearby."

Joe sighed. "If we don't get off this island, we'll never find it," he reminded the others. "Let's spread out the rest of these papers to dry, and then get the chair stuffing out in the sun, too."

They waited hopefully throughout the day for their distress signal to be noticed, but no one appeared. Finally, when evening came, the three boys carried the stuffing, the papers, and pieces of the wooden chair-frame to the highest point on the rocks. A starlit sky spread overhead, but a hard wind and a heavy sea had set in. The high-dashing spray was caught by the wind and whipped over the little island like gusts of fine rain. While Frank and Chet acted as shields, Joe lighted one of their few remaining matches. A feeble flame began to lick at the crumpled papers, only to be extinguished by the driving spray. Another match was used, with the same result.

"Shall we use our last two matches?" Joe asked.

"Try one more," Frank answered.

This time a bluish-yellow finger of flame climbed, spread out, caught at the chair stuffing, and began to lick at the wood.

At that moment a shout, followed by the sudden roar of a motor, brought the boys to their feet.

"It came from the jetty!" cried Joe.

Racing around the lighthouse, they saw a dark figure leap into a motorboat, which then churned out from the island.

Frank and Joe ran at top speed to the end of the stone dock, plunged into the rough water, and struck out after the fleeing boat.

For a while the heavy waves slowed the boat more than the swimmers. But just as Joe came within grabbing distance, it suddenly spurted ahead and roared off into the darkness.

"*Where* was that guy hiding?" Frank asked himself dismally.

Thoroughly soaked and chattering with cold, the Hardys returned to their fire, only to find darkness.

"I did my best to keep it alive," Chet apologized.

The heavy spray had quenched the flames, and the high wind had scattered the remaining paper all over the wet rocks.

CHAPTER VII

Amusement Park Trouble

MISERABLY, the three boys plodded back to the shelter of the lighthouse. Hunger and the lack of dry clothes combined to make a fitful night's sleep. Next day, as the marooned trio stepped into the morning sunlight, a faint droning sound alerted them to a silvery object passing high overhead.

"A seaplane!" Joe cried wildly. "Hey! Help!"

Stripping off their shirts, Frank and Joe waved madly, while Chet bellowed at the top of his lungs. The plane continued toward the mainland.

"No breakfast ration today, boys," Chet said grimly. "No cookies, no water. I won't put up with it. There are fish in this ocean, and I'm going to get one somehow!"

While the stout boy lumbered off with a determined frown, Frank and Joe discussed the case once more.

"Who's trying to get rid of us?" asked Frank. "Blackstone? Then he sure *will* go to any length to keep Bart from proving the rumor."

"It must be Blackstone," Joe decided. "He deliberately let us think Rand was out here. He must have faked that note."

"He *could* have been fooled by it," Frank commented. "Who else might have guessed we'd come here? Cutter? Stewart? The boat owner?"

"Maybe Cutter and Stewart," Joe agreed. "That pale-faced Cutter seems mighty interested in us. Maybe he's working for Blackstone."

A shout from Chet interrupted their speculations. Dripping wet, the stout boy hustled toward them. In his arms gleamed a big mackerel!

"It was washed into a tide pool," he cried excitedly. "I waded in after it!"

A few minutes were enough to rip out part of the railing of the wooden staircase and build a fire. "Here goes my last match," said Chet. Soon he had planked the mackerel in fine style. Using sea water for salt, the boys regaled themselves on the tasty fish.

As they finished, a drone overhead announced the return of the silver seaplane. The boys signaled frantically. This time the craft circled once, then settled down on the calm water.

"Hot dog!" yelled Chet in fervent relief.

The seaplane taxied up to the stone dock, and the cabin door opened. "Hello, there," called the slim, sunburned young pilot, leaning out. "I didn't see your signals earlier, but my passenger did. He didn't tell me until we landed—thought it was a joke."

"Some joke!" said Chet as the boys clambered in.

"Figured I'd better check," said the pilot. "My name's Al West. I'll take you to Larchmont Airport and drive you to town, if that'll help."

"Thanks a million!" Joe said gratefully.

"Same here!" Frank exclaimed. "We thought we were stuck on that rock pile for good!"

Exactly one hour later the Hardys and Chet, who was still shirtless, stepped from Al West's car, waved good-by, and trooped into the *Larchmont Record* office.

Bart Worth stared at them, flabbergasted, and upon hearing their story, expressed still further amazement. "You come home with me for a change of clothes and a solid meal," he ordered. "And you'd better forget my case. This newspaper isn't worth risking your lives."

"We'll accept that meal," Frank answered for the three, "but if you think anything could keep us from this job now, you're mistaken. We have several scores of our own to settle."

While the hungry youths feasted at Worth's bountiful table, the editor paced the floor.

"The lawsuit against me is coming up for trial, and I haven't a shred of proof that some outsider tampered with my editorial," he said. "Jenny Shringle first told me that story. She may have something to back it up, if we could find her."

"*Somebody* besides her neighbor must have seen her leave," Frank reasoned. "We'll comb the town."

"Good!" said Worth. "I'll come along."

The boys set out, accompanied by the editor. First, Chet bought a blazing yellow shirt with a pattern of zigzag lightning on it.

"This'll make a swell distress signal"—he grinned—"if we need one again."

They started from the town square and questioned everyone who might have noticed the seamstress departing a few mornings before. No one had. Gradually the four worked their way to the docks, where the man from whom the boys had rented the boat eyed them suspiciously.

"Where's my boat?" he asked.

"Drifted off," Frank answered.

"Drifted off! Then you all will pay for her!"

Bart Worth immediately drew out his checkbook. "You boys were working in my interest when you lost it," he insisted, despite the Hardys' protests.

Once more they pressed the search. Suddenly Frank halted before a small gift shop not far from the docks.

"Those two oriental vases," he said, pointing to the window. "They're the same kind as the one Blackstone used to hit Rand!"

Eagerly the party went into the store. Chet noticed a small, shy-looking Negro boy, who had been tagging them constantly, enter after them.

"Oh, those china vases," the shopkeeper said in answer to Frank's question. "Yes, they're always sold in pairs."

"That explains how Blackstone replaced his," Frank murmured to the others, as they turned to go. Quickly the little lad slipped out in front of them.

"That kid's been eavesdropping on us for half an hour," Chet finally remarked.

"That youngster?" Bart shook his head doubtfully. "He's doing no harm, I'm sure."

Next, the Hardys and their friends stopped at an open-air fish market. While Frank, Joe, and Bart questioned the paunchy vendor, Chet watched the little boy sneak up behind the high wheel of a loaded cart of fish, and listen with bright, inquisitive eyes.

"Jenny Shringle?" the vendor repeated. "Sure, I saw her. Just the other day, early—"

Crash! Chet had made a frantic dive at the little eavesdropper. The boy had dodged nimbly, but Chet had caused the whole cartload of fresh, wet fish to tip forward on its two wheels. The fish cascaded in a heap on top of Chet!

"My fish!" cried the vendor.

"My new shirt!" Chet wailed.

"Get that kid!" cried Joe to others on the street. But the little boy disappeared.

After Chet had been helped to his feet, and the Hardys had paid for the fish, the vendor, mollified, went on with his story.

"I was settin' up my stall t'other morning. Pretty soon I saw Jenny come by and get on the six-o'clock bus for Sea City. She's got kin there, you know, Mr. Worth. Right funny, though, she didn't carry a suitcase."

"That settles it," said Frank with satisfaction. "We're off for Sea City!"

They hurried back to the *Record's* parking lot, where the four got into Worth's green sedan and sped out to the boys' camp among the dunes. Here Chet quickly changed his fishy shirt, and the party drove off.

They traveled at the highest legal speed toward Sea City. Suddenly Bart slowed down.

"That parked car back there on the shoulder!" he exclaimed. "Professor Rand was in it!"

"Really?" asked Frank, amazed. "Cutter was at the wheel!"

Impatiently Bart sped forward looking for a chance to turn back, but traffic was heavy in both directions. At last he found a chance, but when they retraced their route to the spot, the parked car was gone.

"You're sure it was Rand?" Frank asked as they headed for Sea City once more.

"Yes," Worth stated. "He saw me, too."

"Well, why doesn't he want anyone to know he's still around?" Joe wondered.

Nobody could answer this question. When they reached the main street of Sea City, Frank hopped out and went into a drugstore with a phone booth.

Returning, he reported, "Only one Shringle listed in the telephone book," and gave Bart the address.

Soon they pulled up before a little white bungalow on a side street. The Hardys and Bart alighted and knocked on the door.

A bald, middle-aged man answered. "Oh, you all want to see my cousin Jenny?" he said. "Yes, she's staying here, but she's gone for the day to the amusement park on the boardwalk."

Now the trail was getting hot! When they reached the amusement section, Bart parked his car, and the four walked onto the crowded boardwalk.

It was just after lunchtime. Crowds of vacationers were just leaving a cluster of tables shaded by great beach umbrellas near a boardwalk restaurant.

"There!" cried Bart, pointing.

A middle-aged woman with gray hair was seated at one of the tables. She was sipping an ice-cream soda. As Worth called to her, she looked up at him. Instantly she jumped up, grasped a black purse, and scuttled away.

"Jenny! Wait!" called the editor, as he and the boys dashed after her.

With surprising speed, Jenny Shringle dodged in and out of the throng. Frank gained on her.

"Miss Shringle!" he cried out.

She glanced back with a panicky look but did not slow down.

Suddenly she darted off the walk and halted at one of the amusement ticket windows. The next minute the four friends, running toward her, saw her disappear into a brightly painted "fun house" billed as *Bluebeard's Palace*.

At one side of the high, bizarre building, a well-greased wooden slide shot the screaming customers down to the boardwalk.

Chet folded his arms. "Well," he said, "all we do is wait here till Jenny Shringle comes out. She can't stay in there forever."

Bart shook his head. "This fun house is too rough for a woman of Jenny's age."

"We'd better go in," Frank agreed, "before she gets hurt. Bart, you wait here."

He quickly purchased admission tickets, and the three boys entered the fun house. Frank led the way through a dark, narrow tunnel. Chet followed, then Joe.

As fast as possible, they stumbled forward. Weird screams startled them. Hanging cobwebs brushed their faces. Slithery, snakelike forms writhed underfoot. Finally reaching a level place, they walked ahead rapidly—only to find themselves on a treadmill carrying them backward!

At last, Frank, stepping off the treadmill after the others, entered a dimly lighted chamber with distortion mirrors around the walls.

Suddenly he stopped short. Confronting him was a wide-shouldered, giant figure with a very narrow waist. Frank burst out laughing. It was his own image, greatly exaggerated! Then, reflected behind him loomed another figure of gorilla-like proportions, with a familiar flattened face.

"I warned you!" a hoarse voice rasped.

As the huge arms grabbed for him, Frank ducked nimbly into the next room. In the weird half-light the boy saw that the floor tilted sideways, and the walls were tipped crazily. Frank found that he was forced to run downhill without being able to stop himself.

In another instant he bowled, helpless, into Chet and Joe, who had just picked themselves up at the far wall. The next second, the heavy bulk of the flat-faced man hurtled into their midst. All four went down on the floor in a heap.

Frank, who had been struck hard in the pit of the stomach, gasped for breath. As the four rolled about in a violent struggle, he caught the gleam of a knife in the big man's hand!

CHAPTER VIII

Campfire Eavesdropper

"Look out!" Frank yelled. "He has a knife!"

The boy threw himself on the man's brawny forearm, seized his wrist, and clung to it grimly.

As their antagonist struggled for a foothold, Joe dived under the blade for an ankle-high tackle. The man smacked heavily into the inclined floor, where Chet pounced on his chest.

All this time Frank had clung to the man's arm. Now he gave the thick wrist a sudden twisting wrench. The man gave a roar of pain. His big fist opened, and the knife slid harmlessly away over the tilted floor.

"This fun house isn't much fun any more!" Joe exclaimed.

Savagely the big man kicked and lashed out. The boys gave hard, chopping blows in return.

New customers paused at the entrance to the tilted chamber. With one desperate heave, the

"Look out!" Frank yelled. "He has a knife!"

flat-faced man shoved the boys aside and fled.

Recovering, Frank, Joe, and Chet plunged into a dark passage in pursuit. Excited screaming reached their ears from the blackness ahead. Suddenly they found themselves clambering on hands and knees, for the passage now sloped sharply upward. Above them appeared a round hole with the bright daylight showing beyond.

"It's the exit with the steep chute!" Joe warned. "Hurry!"

Suddenly the short, pudgy figure of a woman teetered in the opening at the top of the slide.

"Oh, oh!" she shrieked in terror. "Please, somebody please help me!"

Just ahead of the boys the hoarse-voiced man climbed into the light. Hastily he dived for the chute, knocking the frightened woman off balance, and going ahead of her. With a scream, she too began to slide down backward.

Frank, quick as lightning, stretched forward, grabbed the woman, and hauled her back to safety.

"Where's the man?" Joe asked, reaching the top.

"Just went down," Frank answered.

Immediately Joe, followed by Chet, whisked down the chute to continue the chase.

"*I* can't do that!" sobbed the woman.

"It's all right, Miss Shringle," Frank said soothingly. "You are Miss Shringle?" She nodded, as he went on, "There must be a stairway nearby."

As other customers pressed behind them, the boy detected a camouflaged door just beside him. He guided the shaken seamstress through it onto a well-lighted flight of steps. They led down behind the façade of the building.

As Frank, supporting Jenny, returned to the boardwalk, Joe, Chet, and Bart Worth hurried up. "Lost that big guy in the crowd," Joe reported. "How's Miss Shringle?"

"She'll be all right," Frank assured them as he led Miss Shringle to a bench.

"Yes, yes—thank you so much," the seamstress mumbled. But she avoided meeting their eyes—especially Bart Worth's.

"Why did you run away from me, Jenny?" he asked presently.

The woman folded her hands in her lap and stared ahead. "Because—because I'm not allowed to speak to anyone now." She spoke the words defiantly, but there was fear in her voice.

"Not allowed by whom?" the editor prompted. "Did you come here only to visit your cousin?"

The seamstress shook her head emphatically.

"Is it Blackstone—something to do with the rumors you told me about?"

The woman simply pressed her lips together in stony silence.

"All right. Have it your way." Bart sighed. "If you want to freshen up, we'll wait and drive you back to your cousin's."

Miss Shringle nodded and hurried off.

"Anyway, we've learned something," Frank pointed out, "just from the questions she *won't* answer. We know she's trying to keep certain information from us."

"Yes. The name Blackstone is the signal for Jenny to clam up completely," Joe remarked.

"Did you notice her dress?" Frank went on. "It was new—nothing like the 'best dress' her neighbor described. The same with her handbag and hat. Somebody paid her to get out of Larchmont and keep still!"

"Blackstone," Worth put in with satisfaction. "It must mean he knows my story can be proved!"

Riding back to her cousin's with them, Jenny Shringle preserved an obstinate silence.

"Jenny, you've *got* to understand how serious this is," the editor pleaded. "Professor Rand disappeared right after these boys saw Blackstone strike him during an argument."

"That's right," Frank said. "Yet, when we brought back the police for a search of Blackstone's place, your former employer showed us a friendly note from the professor—to prove the two of them are on good terms."

A flicker of surprise showed in the woman's gray eyes. Abruptly she addressed Frank.

"You helped me," she said, "so I'll tell you this much. In all the thirty years I worked in that house, the Blackstones had nothing to do with the

Rands. Oh, they weren't feuding. They just ignored each other—never even sent greeting cards. Ruel Rand would as soon write Blackstone a friendly note as jump into that pond I heard them quarreling about!"

"Then you don't think Rand wrote it?" Frank asked as he escorted the woman up to her cousin's little white house.

"Impossible," said Jenny, slipping inside.

In thoughtful silence the young detectives and their client drove back to Larchmont. Night had fallen before they reached the high dunes around the campsite. As the sound of Bart's car died away on the road back to town, the boys busied themselves with supper preparations.

The camp stove was lighted. Meanwhile, Chet broke a dozen eggs into a bowl and beat them furiously. Joe heated a greased deep skillet over the flame. While the Hardys watched, Chet poured his omelet mixture, muttering all the time like a witch over her brew.

"Ah . . . bits of ham—so. Chopped onions . . . potatoes . . . salt . . . Now, with the turner, flip!"

A few minutes later, each boy was balancing a tin plate filled with a huge steaming third of the puffy omelet, and eating by flashlight.

Finishing, Chet gave a sigh of appeased hunger. At that moment, in the rays of the light, Joe saw a pair of white eyes in a dark face. Quickly he signaled the others to remain still. After a moment, the face disappeared.

"It's the boy who was cavesdropping on us today," Joe whispered. "Now our campsite is known." He and Frank decided to trail the lad.

The small figure proved easy to follow among the dunes, for the moonlight was already bright.

"He's carrying a package," Frank noted.

The boy had struck across the sand toward the pond. With the help of the moon, the young sleuths kept him in sight all the way.

"He's heading for the Rand place," Joe observed as the lad turned left at the pond.

The little boy, however, merely skirted the water and went into the swamp.

"I'll bet he knows we're following him," whispered Frank. "He's trying to throw us off."

The lad took the same trail over which the Hardys had chased the tall figure in the long coat a few nights before. The hedge loomed up at the end of the path. The boy disappeared through it.

"Let's wait here," Frank suggested. "He'll think he's rid of us and come back."

The brothers crouched behind a bush. Presently a light rustling in the hedge alerted them. In a moment the small boy passed by them. Without his package, he scuttled alongside the pond and over to the Blackstone property. Frank and Joe saw him pause near the big house and look back. Then he vanished into its cellar.

"That's funny. He sure knows his way around here. Wonder who he is," Frank muttered.

"Mysterious character number seven." Joe chuckled. "Let's have another look at the pond."

Noiselessly the two boys walked on until they reached the westerly edge of the still water. Suddenly, in the moonlight, a ripple marred the surface very near them.

"The monster!" Joe whispered excitedly.

The saw-tooth fin emerged eerily in the moonlight. The huge creature remained visible for a few seconds, then slipped out of sight into the depths of the pond.

"Back to camp," Joe said excitedly. "We'll get our diving gear and bring underwater lights. We'll find out what that thing is yet!"

"Right," Frank agreed. "Let's cut through Blackstone's property and go to the beach that way. It'll be easier going, and we'll save time."

When the Hardys reached the wealthy man's well-kept yards, they silently sprinted across the dark lawns, keeping away from the lighted house. But as they raced toward the beach, two enormous, bounding black shapes suddenly flew at them from the side. Blackstone's two ferocious watchdogs had been turned loose!

With a vicious snarl, the larger of the police dogs leaped at Frank and knocked him to the ground.

CHAPTER IX

Fishing Boat Clue

THE huge dog bared its teeth as it hovered over Frank. Rolling to the side, he seized the animal's throat to hold the fangs away from his body.

Joe had already whipped off his sweat shirt. He rushed in and bagged the dog's head with it.

While the baffled animal leaped about, giving short, confused barks, the brothers sprinted toward the ocean. They expected the smaller dog to streak after them, but it remained with its pal.

"That was close!" Joe panted. "You okay, Frank?"

"Yes, but I sure had a good scare. Say, wonder if somebody inside told Mr. Blackstone we were around, and he deliberately set his dogs on us."

"Wouldn't put it past him," Joe grumbled.

In camp once more, the young sleuths told Chet

their plan, then loaded aqualungs, masks, weighted belts, Frank's flippers, and underwater lights into rucksacks. With Chet carrying their fishing spears, they set out for the pond.

To avoid Blackstone's dogs, the boys went by way of the tangled underbrush directly to the pond. The Hardys rigged themselves out for their plunge. Each brother grasped a spear in one hand and an underwater lamp in the other.

"Chet," Frank said, "if anybody comes, or if you see that monster surface, knock two stones together under water to warn us."

"Check."

The two divers submerged. For a while Chet could see their lamps moving in ever-widening arcs away from him. Soon the lights grew dim and finally vanished altogether. Chet felt very much alone with the gloomy swamp across the pond, a mysterious, deserted mansion to his left, and fierce dogs to his right.

A splash startled him. An unearthly looking creature suddenly reared up from the water close by and came toward him.

"Yi! Help!" he bellowed.

"Keep still, for Pete's sake!" came Joe's calm voice. "I got some mud on me, that's all."

Soon Frank, also looking like some sort of monster in his mud-covered equipment, waded ashore.

"Nothing," he reported. "No sign of the prehistoric critter. We covered the whole pond."

Quickly the brothers washed and dressed. Shouldering their packs, they hiked back to camp for a well-earned night's rest.

In the bright sunshine of the next morning, the waves rolled in from the blue Atlantic. Frank and Joe, in bathing trunks, dashed across the beach and dived into the breakers.

"Terrific!" Joe yelled, riding in on the crest of a wave. "Where's Chet?"

"Getting breakfast!" Frank shouted as he swam. "Since when can he wait to eat?"

Suddenly Frank swam over to Joe. "There's that fishing smack again," he said, glancing seaward. "It's closer this morning."

Joe nodded. "I just realized that boat's been out there ever since the morning after we set up camp. Once in a while I've spotted a figure on deck, but mostly the boat looks deserted." Suddenly he stared at his brother. "You don't think somebody's anchored out there to spy on us?"

"That's a good hunch," Frank answered as the boys swam ashore. "Let's look into it later," he proposed. "First, though, we'd better see if we can locate Grover or Professor Rand. I'm convinced both know something important to Bart's case."

Later, as the chums ate breakfast, Frank said, "I wonder if that little boy is a relative of Grover's, and was taking that package to him?"

"Mm." Joe pondered this. "What do you suppose was in the package?"

"Food," Chet said promptly. "What else?"

Though the Hardys laughed, they considered Chet's conclusion a good one. "If Grover is in hiding for some reason," Frank said, "maybe the little boy brings him his meals. Let's go over to Professor Rand's this morning and scout around that hedge."

An hour later Joe was slipping through the hedge opening where the Negro boy had disappeared the night before. He slid down to the meadow beneath. Frank and Chet followed.

Once in the field, they saw that the high bank of shrubbery extended from the back of the old mansion deep into the swamp. The boys moved along the base of the seven-foot rise toward the house.

A thick blackberry patch choked the end of the meadow. Picking and eating the fruit as he tramped through the patch, Chet suddenly called out, "Say, here are some bricks, fellows. Looks like a chimney. And here's a corroded copper pot. Must be the ruins of an old kitchen."

"That's it!" Frank cried, running over.

"What?" Joe asked.

"We're right behind the big house," his brother pointed out. "Chet has just found the remains of the old plantation kitchen."

"So?"

"That's how the prowler in the long coat vanished! There must be an underground passage from this spot to the house which was used for carrying the cooked food in olden days."

"Come on!" cried Joe. "Let's find it!"

Carefully the boys scoured the surrounding terrain, but they saw no evidence of any passage.

"We'll come back tonight," Joe proposed, "and watch for the little boy. He'll lead us to it."

"Right," Frank said. "Our next move is to investigate the fishing smack."

Once more the friends returned to camp. After lunch they mapped out careful plans for their sleuthing maneuvers. Then the Hardys piled their skin-diving gear into the yellow convertible and, with Chet, drove to the Larchmont docks.

"Another boat!" repeated the man at the boat livery. "Why, you fellers didn't bring back the first one you rented!"

"We will this time," Frank assured him. "We'd like to buy some fishing tackle and bait, too."

The transactions were completed. Soon the young detectives were chugging over the blue-green water past the buoys. When the boat had left the inlet behind, it turned along the shore line.

As planned, Chet at the wheel guided the craft gradually in the direction of the fishing smack. Meanwhile, Frank and Joe put on their diving gear and lay down out of sight below the gunwales. Presently Chet anchored a few hundred yards from the suspicious fishing vessel. Quietly the Hardys slipped over the side into the ocean, hoping they had not been seen. Nonchalantly the plump boy began to fish.

A short time later Frank and Joe came noiselessly to the surface beside the smack's hull. Treading water, they listened intently as hot, angry voices reached their ears.

"We've given you every opportunity, Jed," came one voice louder and sharper than the others. "You muffed them all. First the warehouse trick, then you wrecked the wrong car. They got away from the lighthouse alive and slipped through your fingers in Sea City. What good does it do for Stewart and me to watch their movements and inform you?"

"I couldn't help it," complained a familiar hoarse voice. "Those kids are a tougher job than I expected."

Excitedly Joe whispered, "So the flat-faced guy is named Jed—and he's in cahoots with Cutter!"

Frank nodded tensely. The argument aboard continued. "Well, see that you don't fail next time," barked Cutter. "We'll never get what we want if we don't stop those meddling snoopers!"

The speakers lowered their voices, making it impossible for the boys to hear more. Submerging, Frank and Joe stroked back to their own boat.

"Boy, have I got fish," Chet announced proudly

as he helped his friends aboard. "Look at these!"

"We made a catch, too." Joe told him what they had overheard at the fishing vessel as the little boat chugged back to harbor.

"All of which means," Frank added, "that Cutter *is* out to get us, and that hoarse-voiced fellow is in league with him, and was the 'ghost' on Storm Island!"

Chet looked mystified. "You think Cutter's antique business is just a cover-up and he's in Blackstone's pay?"

"Could be," Frank replied. "Also, he could be in Rand's pay, for that matter. Though I still have a hunch the professor isn't a crook. Maybe Cutter's working some game of his own."

After returning the boat, the boys drove straight back to the dunes.

"Out of the way!" Chet ordered as the Hardys offered to help with supper. "These are special fish. Ole Chet caught 'em, Ole Chet will cook 'em, and Ole Chet will serve 'em!"

"Okay." Frank laughed. "Just so Old Chet doesn't do all the eating, too."

"Time to work!" Joe grinned, as they finished supper. "On we go to Professor Rand's."

Though it was still daylight, the boys took their flashlights and set off. When they reached the meadow, they hid in the berry patch and settled down to wait for the little Negro boy to appear.

Frank's eyes narrowed as he scrutinized the surrounding area. "You know," he whispered, "these old kitchen fragments may have been moved here. This may not have been a kitchen at all. Let's try those other bushes—at the base of the bank."

"Good deduction," said Joe.

The youths arose and searched carefully behind the thick screen of brush Frank had pointed out.

"Here!" Joe signaled, his fingers touching a stone frame set into the steep rise under the hedge. The other boys joined him.

Elatedly, the three stared at a heavy wooden door. "The entrance to the passageway, I'll bet!" Chet exclaimed.

"*Sh!*" Frank warned. "Someone's coming!"

The three shrank into the bushes and waited breathlessly. There was faint rustling, and the little boy came by with a newspaper-wrapped package. He went through the door!

As soon as they dared, Frank, Joe, and Chet noiselessly followed, and entered a dark brick-walled passageway. Ahead and to their left, a dim shaft of light knifed into the darkness, then vanished as the small boy went through a low door.

The youths crept forward. Chet and Joe tensed expectantly as Frank placed his hand on the door ready to shove it inward.

"Here goes!" he whispered.

CHAPTER X

Hidden Passageway

AT FRANK's push the heavy door swung inward and banged against the wall.

"Oh—oh—go away, sir. Go away!" sang out a child's clear voice.

The Hardys and Chet stared in astonishment at the scene before them. The yellow light of a kerosene lamp on a small wooden table revealed the seated figures of the little Negro boy and the old servant, Grover. In the man's hands, partially opened, was the small package, containing meat and bread.

In his confusion the lad almost tipped over backward in his chair. He leaped up and scampered into the shadows of several huge wooden barrels ranged sideways upon racks.

But the elderly man stood up calmly and faced the boys across the glass chimney of the lamp. "What is it you want?" he asked in a low voice.

"You must know, Grover," Frank answered as Joe and Chet stepped into the light. "You saw Mr. Blackstone strike Professor Rand, and you saw us come to ask about it. We know there's something peculiar going on, and we are trying to find out what it is."

"I'm not talking to you." The thin old man's eyes flashed in sudden anger. "You've got no business here. Timmy!" He turned to the lad. "Did you show these folks where to find me?"

An eye and a forehead peered around a cask. "No, Grandpa," came Timmy's small voice.

"You come on out here," Grover ordered. "We've been found. There'll be a heap of trouble for you and me now."

"We're sorry," Frank said kindly, as the little boy crept timidly to his grandfather's side. "We don't intend any harm. I don't think you realize how important it is for us to talk to you. Somebody's been trying to kill us, or at least scare us off this case. Professor Rand might tell us why, but he has evidently disappeared. Unless you help us, we haven't a chance of straightening things out."

As briefly as possible, Frank explained to the elderly retainer why the boys had come to Larchmont. While he spoke, the old servant watched him closely. The anger faded from his eyes, and the lines of his face deepened with concern.

"I just knew, if they started that feud up again

there wasn't any good going to come of it!"
Grover sighed. "All right, sir, I'll tell you folks
what I can. I don't like trouble. The faster everything's cleared up, the happier lots of folks
will be."

"Did Mr. Blackstone send you here to hide
from us?" Joe queried.

"Yes, sir, he did," Grover admitted. "From Mr.
Worth, too. And he sent Miss Shringle some
money to go off and visit her relatives."

"So you were here the whole time, instead of
in Chicago," Joe continued.

"Mr. Blackstone wanted me to go out there,"
Grover admitted. "But when a body gets as old as
I am, he's kind of scared to ride in trains or air-
planes way off a thousand miles away from where
he's been living all his life. So I said I'd keep
snug in this beverage room, instead. I suppose
you guessed this is the old plantation kitchen passage. Both sides of the family know about it."

"You've been with the Blackstones a long
time?" Chet spoke up.

"All my life, sir. My father served the Blackstones, and *his* father did, too. Used to be a grand
family, way back."

"But *why* did this Mr. Blackstone make you
hide out?" Joe prompted. "Because we'd ask you
about the quarrel we saw?"

"Yes. The two gentlemen are fighting over that
pond again. But somehow they don't want people

to *know* they're fighting over it. Soon as Mr. Blackstone hit Mr. Rand with that vase, I switched off the lights—in case somebody was watching."

"But how did you cover it up so fast?" Joe wondered.

"Oh, Mr. Blackstone and I carried Professor Rand into the next room. Then we swept the broken pieces of the vase under a rug. Mr. Blackstone put on his relaxing jacket and set that twin vase on his desk. He opened up his book. Then I went and let you boys in."

"Professor Rand's all right, then?" Frank inquired.

"Yes, he came round after an hour, mad as a wet hen. Couldn't complain much though, because they didn't want to attract anybody's attention about their arguing over the land. After Professor Rand left, Mr. Blackstone said that he wanted me to go to Chicago for a while."

"Do you know where the professor is staying?" Frank asked.

Grover shrugged. "If he's gone, *I* don't know where he's keepin' himself. Timmy, have you seen Mr. Rand around lately?"

"No, Grandpa," replied the lad meekly. With round eyes, he watched the boys.

"Timmy's been sort of shadowing you," the old man explained. "He was afraid you'd make trouble for me if you found me." Grover smiled at his grandson. "These gentlemen are all right, Timmy. No need to fear."

At this point Joe decided to try a new lead. "Grover," he began, "do you know *why* the Rands and Blackstones are fighting over the border line property again? Is it because the Blackstone family fortune is buried on it somewhere?"

"Also, where's Hidden Harbor?" Frank added.

For a moment Grover blinked at the boys in amazement. "How'd you all know about that?"

Quickly Joe recounted the discovery of the captain's note while the boys were marooned at the lighthouse.

"You all know about as much about it as I do," Grover informed them. "Old Mr. Clement Blackstone, they say, buried his money and family papers before he sailed away to England. That was while the Civil War was going on. Mr. Clement never came back. He died over there—after the war. Then the Rands and Blackstones started feuding about that land."

"Where was the treasure buried, exactly?" Joe pursued. "Didn't anybody ever dig it up?"

"Seems they kind of lost track of things, somehow," the old man answered, obviously puzzled himself. "My daddy told me when I was a boy *he* once heard it was buried at the mouth of Hidden Harbor, but I don't know any Hidden Harbor."

"Hmm, that's something new, anyhow," Joe observed. "At the *mouth* of the harbor."

"It's the key to the whole case," Frank declared earnestly. "Not the money, but the papers. They'll tell us how the fortune was made. They might prove Bart's story!"

After a moment's reflection, he injected a new idea. "You say everybody 'lost track' of the fortune, Grover," Frank said. "Didn't the feud die down just about the same time? There must be some connection."

"You mean," Joe put in, "both families wanted the disputed land in order to locate Clement's buried fortune. But after they 'lost track' of it, the land wasn't important to them any more?"

"Right," Frank said. "The feud has started up again because somebody found a clue to the fortune."

"I can't be rightly sure," Grover suddenly declared, "but it seems to me Professor Rand is kind of looking for that money. Fact is, he was the one started up this feuding. Mr. Blackstone, he's a rich man—he doesn't need any more money than he's got. But Mr. Rand—well, you boys have seen his house. He sure could use a fortune."

"That's a logical idea," Joe agreed.

"Then what is Blackstone making such a fuss about?" demanded Chet, bewildered.

"Oh, Blackstone may not want the money," Joe pointed out. "It's those family papers he doesn't want found, because they contain proof of something he doesn't want publicized."

"I get it! The piracy and smuggling charges!"
Chet exclaimed. "The evidence Bart needs!"

Frank nodded decisively. "All this boils down
to one thing, fellows: We must find Hidden Harbor and find it fast, before Bart's case comes to
court!"

Suddenly Joe held up his hand, warning for silence. From outside the room, the sound of
leather heels striking upon brick reached them.

"Somebody's comin' down the passage," Grover
whispered nervously.

Quickly the old man bent over the lamp chimney and gave a strong puff. The old beverage
room was plunged into total darkness. The footsteps passed by, unhurried, in the direction of
the plantation house.

"Who could it be?" Frank asked Grover.

"I don't know, sir," was the answer. "Nobody
knows this place except the family and the servants."

"Joe, you and I will follow that man!" Frank
decided quickly. "Chet, stay out in the passage by
this room. Just make sure the fellow doesn't slip
back and escape."

Cautiously Frank pulled back the door, and the
three slipped into the dark passageway. Ahead,
the footsteps sounded on the brick floor with a
regular, hollow ring.

"Knows his way," Joe murmured as the brothers crept along in pursuit.

Abruptly the sharp heel taps ceased. A moment later came a steady scraping sound.

"He's climbing stairs," whispered Frank.

Hurrying forward, the young sleuths found that the passage branched into two corridors. One led to a narrow brick stairway.

"Must go to the second story," Frank deduced. "The other branch probably leads to the kitchen of the house."

Afraid to turn on their flashes lest they be detected, the boys mounted the steps. A narrow slit of light indicated a door slightly ajar above them. After listening carefully a moment, Frank pushed it lightly, and he and Joe stepped into an empty closet.

At the front of the closet was another door, opened a crack. Warily, the brothers stepped into a lamplit room.

As the young detectives looked curiously around them, a sudden sound on their right caused them to whirl sharply.

The hall door to the room they had entered was just closing. The Hardys heard the metallic click of a key turning, and a lock bar sliding into place.

Fearing trouble, Joe raced to the tunnel entrance. It was locked.

CHAPTER XI

Acrobatic Detectives

"Locked in!" exclaimed Joe, rattling the door handle. "What's the idea?" He and Frank heard the booted footsteps retreating along the hall and down a stairway.

The boys surveyed their little prison. A narrow bed and broad writing table were the extent of the furniture, except for well-stocked bookshelves that covered two walls from floor to ceiling.

"This must be Professor Rand's study," Frank whispered. He examined the volumes briefly. "They're all on ancient Indian civilizations," he noted. "And look! Here are some written by Professor Rand."

"Very interesting," Joe said wryly. "Right now I'm more interested in getting out of here."

"Let's try the window," proposed Frank.

He pulled open two narrow french doors. A gust of cold wind from the sea struck the boys as they stepped onto a railed balcony.

"No ground supports," Joe noted, leaning out over the rail. "We're too high to jump."

The brothers looked around from their perch, located on the front face of the mansion. The huge trees were out of reach, as was the roof above them.

Suddenly, below them, the Hardys distinctly heard the sound of a door closing.

"Over there!" Joe pointed toward a tall man's figure. The man paused to jerk a flashlight from his pocket. In the same motion, something white fluttered to the ground. Then the man, carrying a spade, slipped around the corner of the house.

"Must be Professor Rand!" Joe hissed excitedly. "I wish we could get hold of that paper he dropped."

Frank nodded. "Wonder if *he* locked us in."

Just then a swift gust of wind carried the white square upward. It wavered, and spiraled around directly toward the boys!

The Hardys clutched and pawed the air. Maddeningly the paper swooped high, sideslipped, and landed on another little balcony two window widths from their own.

"Too far to jump," Frank judged. "See if we can bridge it. We must get that paper. I've a hunch it's important!" he declared grimly.

They stepped over the top rail together. As Frank wedged his toes under the bottom rail and grasped the lower sections of two of the sturdy spindles, Joe, facing outward, bent down and took hold of his brother's ankles.

"Ready!" he called.

Frank loosened his foothold but held fast to the spindles as Joe gave a mighty swing, carrying both boys into the air. Joe, finding he could reach the next balcony, hooked his knees over its railing, let go his grip on Frank, and pulled himself up. But just as he stepped to safety, a fresh gust of wind whirled the white paper upward and away.

The paper sailed farther and farther. Finally it disappeared around the corner of the house.

Now, trying the french windows on his own balcony, Joe found them locked securely. The boys groaned and Frank said, "This would have been a swell time to follow the fellow in the raincoat."

"I'll bet he locked us in," Joe reasoned. "He left the secret door through the closet open and the light on in the study, to trap us."

Frank had another theory. "Maybe it *wasn't* Rand whose steps we heard. Someone *else* could've set the trap. The professor might've been here the whole time and never realized what was going on."

Suddenly, between rushes of wind, a faint

whistling came to the boys' ears from the grounds.

Who could that be? the Hardys wondered.

Again the whistling came. Then a white-shirted figure crept cautiously out in front of the house.

"Chet!" called Frank with relief.

"Here I am," came the reply. "Got tired of waiting in that old passage. What are you two doing up there, anyhow?"

"We're locked out," Joe told him. "See if you can get into the house and free us."

The stout boy marched up to the front door, and tried it. "Locked," he muttered. Almost automatically he stooped and looked under the mat. "Yes. Here we are—a key."

Inserting it in the lock, Chet opened the heavy door and vanished inside. In two minutes he freed Joe, then Frank. "That was easy," he said. "Where do we go now?"

"Back outside," Frank answered. "We have a flying clue to bring down!"

After bolting the room door, the three raced downstairs, locked the front door, replaced the key, and ran around the house. By now the dusk had deepened.

"No flashlights," said Frank. "We'll have a better chance to see the paper against a dark background."

Frank turned his gaze upward. "There it is!" he announced.

High in the wisteria covering the wide chimney, fluttered the white square of paper.

"Oh-h," moaned Chet. "Three of us standing on each other's shoulders couldn't reach *that* high."

"No, but if the top man had a stick, he might," Frank pointed out.

While Chet and Frank kept watch on the unpredictable paper, Joe found a fallen branch.

"You're elected anchor man, Chet," Joe said, returning. Frank hauled himself up to stand on the stout boy's shoulders. Then Joe hoisted himself up onto his brother's. He clutched the wisteria vine for balance and began to fish upward with the stick.

"Can't . . . reach it." Joe grunted, extending to his utmost length.

"You're stepping on my ear," warned Frank.

In desperation, Joe took aim and flung his branch upward. With a rustling of leaves, the paper came free. The human ladder collapsed, the Hardys breaking their fall by somersaulting. The trio dashed after the white square, which now sailed toward the back of the house.

Here the wind was not so strong. The paper lost altitude, and Joe, rushing up with a cry of triumph, made a neat two-handed catch.

While Chet held his flashlight, the Hardys examined their find. Two sheets of white paper were stapled together. The one on top appeared to be a carefully hand-drawn map.

"It's the Rand property," said Frank. "Here's the house, with the pond and swamp behind. But what's this encircled area?" Squinting closer, he read the small printed words which covered the pond and part of the swamp:

SITE OF ANCIENT INDIAN VILLAGE

"What's on the second page?" Joe asked.

"It's a letter to Professor Rand from State University," Frank reported, after scanning the document briefly. "It says they have no funds for excavation of the site indicated, without more proof that something of archaeological value exists."

"So *that's* what Rand wants to find!" Joe exclaimed. "An ancient Indian village—not the buried family fortune!"

"Don't be too sure," Frank cautioned. "He may be trying to kill two birds with one stone. Maybe he wants the money to finance the excavation."

After tucking the two papers in his pocket, Frank led the way toward the pond. A light moved slowly among the big, moss-hung cypresses of the swamp.

As the boys crept nearer, they spotted the tall figure digging, and stooping to examine each spadeful.

"That must be Professor Rand!" Joe whispered. Impetuously he started forward, but Frank pulled his brother back.

"What's the matter? We've been trying to catch up with Rand for days!" Joe argued.

"It's not the right time," Frank countered. "He's doing his best to hide his activities, besides dodging us! Do you think we'd learn anything from him at this point?"

"Well, I guess he wouldn't be very friendly," Joe admitted.

"He'll be more on his guard than ever," Frank went on. "It would be better to let him *think* we've given up. But we'll spy on him, starting right now."

"Still, we can't wait too long," Joe insisted. "The trial against Bart Worth is getting closer, and we haven't turned up the evidence he needs."

All this time the boys had been moving forward and presently were in an advantageous position to watch the digger. To their disappointment the man stopped his work almost immediately, swung the shovel over his shoulder, and started back in the direction from which he had come.

"I guess he's through for tonight, and we didn't learn a thing," Chet complained, sloshing in and out of the mucky swamp.

The digger, familiar with the area, outdistanced them. When the boys reached the Rand house, it was in darkness.

"Let's get back to camp," Chet begged. "I've had it. Besides, there's food back there."

The Hardys, feeling they could learn nothing more at the moment, agreed. Next morning found them driving to Larchmont on a new angle.

"Guess Joe and I will have a history lesson at the library," Frank told Chet, "while you stock up on food."

They stopped at the town's public library and the Hardys went inside. Chet continued on to shop for food. Soon Frank and Joe were engrossed in a thickly bound stack of yellowed newspapers dating back before the Civil War.

"Plenty of piracy and smuggling going on along this coast just before the war," Frank observed.

"Yes," Joe corroborated. "Officials couldn't tell where all the stolen goods and contraband were coming from."

"The name Blackstone seems to have become more and more prominent in business, social, and civic events," Frank went on. "Anything else interesting?"

"This paper reports a tremendous hurricane just after the Civil War ended. Nothing to do with our case, I suppose."

The boys finished their research and left the library. Chet was waiting outside in the convertible.

"Saw Mr. Cutter hanging around the supermarket," he reported. "Think he saw me but didn't let on."

"He's so busy keeping tabs on us he doesn't have time for his own business," Joe stated.

"Why don't *we* trail *him?*"

Frank had another idea. "I think now we ought to look for Hidden Harbor—from the air, where we'll have a better view. The Blackstones could have done all the smuggling mentioned in the newspapers by means of such a secret harbor. That would explain their sudden prosperity, and also why Rand and Blackstone, despite their differences, are so hush-hush over everything."

"You fellows go on," Chet said. "I'll take this stuff back to camp. What'll you do for a plane?"

"Engage Al West," Joe answered. "I'll check with the airport."

The boy made his call from a booth in a store. He learned that the young pilot would be glad to take them up. "Come right over," Al said.

When Joe left, he spotted Mr. Stewart seated in the adjoining booth! "Did he overhear me?" Joe wondered.

Chet drove the convertible back to camp with the supplies, while Frank and Joe hailed the rather antiquated yellow-and-black town taxi. Soon they were heading along the main road to the airport. Frank watched carefully, but nobody seemed to be following them.

At the airport Al greeted the Hardys affably and invited them to lunch in the airport cafeteria. Afterward, the three boarded Al's trim amphibian. Frank sat beside the pilot, Joe behind him in a comfortable leather seat. After getting clearance from the tower, Al gunned the plane down the runway, eased back on the wheel, and they were air-borne. For some minutes the ship gained altitude. Then, without warning, it lurched violently to portside and nosed down.

Frank was thrown against the pilot, who slammed sideways against the cockpit window.

"What's wrong?" Joe shouted.

"Don't know," Frank replied, then suddenly he said, "Al's out cold! We'll crash!"

CHAPTER XII

Alligator!

WITH engines roaring, the amphibian was heading toward the ground at a steep angle.

"Good night!" Joe yelled.

Frank sprang into action. He pushed Al back into the seat with his left arm, seized the wheel with his right hand, and pulled back. No response!

Joe reached forward, grasped Al's shoulders, and straightened the limp pilot in his seat. Frank, with both hands on the wheel now, strained to level the faltering plane. Sweat stood out on his forehead as the wooded swamp beneath them seemed to rush upward.

Barely at treetop level, the craft recovered from its sickening dive.

Al's eyes fluttered open. He shook his head, then he came fully alert as several branches scraped the bottom of his craft. He grasped the wheel from Frank, and with his jaw set grimly, fought for altitude.

Nobody spoke until Al banked toward the airport.

"Thanks," he said, "I think we'll make it."

"What happened?" Joe asked.

"Control failure. Something went haywire."

Al radioed for emergency clearance, and brought the plane in for a rough landing. When they climbed out, shaken by their close brush with death, Al summoned the maintenance crew. Together they went over the controls.

"Here's your trouble," one of the mechanics said finally. "A stabilizer cable has been cut!"

"Sabotage!" Joe exclaimed.

Frank nodded understandingly. "Stewart must've heard you telephone the airport. But how did he have time to get here and cut the cable before we arrived?"

Joe, seeing a puzzled look on Al's face, told him of Cutter's and Stewart's apparent attempts on the boys' lives.

The pilot frowned. "What road did you take out here?" he asked.

"The main highway from Larchmont."

"There's a shorter way, over back roads. That old taxi probably crawled like a snail, too. Stewart could easily have beaten you here, and tampered with the ship while we ate lunch."

Al brought out his tool kit and quickly fixed

the damaged cable. He threw a calculating glance at the sky, where dark clouds were forming in the west.

"Storm's coming up," he said. "But I guess we still have time to look around before it hits."

Once more, the silver amphibian raced down the runway and lifted into the air.

"I hope Chet nails things down at camp," Frank remarked.

"He'd better. Haven't you heard?" Al asked. "Hurricane warnings have been out since last night. There's a big one working up from the Gulf of Mexico, but she shouldn't arrive here for several hours."

The craft passed high over Larchmont, then winged above the ocean. The choppy water was a deep, black-tinged green. White lines of foam stroked far up on the beach.

"There's our tent!" Joe called out.

"Yes, and there's our enemy's observation post." Frank pointed to the fishing smack bobbing at anchor on the rough water.

Al West banked the ship inland across the pale, high-peaked sand dunes. From this height, all the huge ancestral Blackstone plantation was visible at once. On the right, the shiny slates of Samuel Blackstone's home peeped through well-spaced trees. Rand's mansion, nearly overgrown, was harder to pick out. Between the two houses, the pond reflected the troubled gray sky. At the edge of the water on the ocean side, black-cypress foliage indicated the swampland.

"You say you're looking for a harbor?" Al was perplexed. "A harbor means a break in the coast, fellows. It's solid beach and dunes along here."

Frank was eying the fingers of water leading from the pond, some wide, some narrow, which lost themselves among the dunes or stretched into the swamp among the cypresses.

"Go lower, Al," Frank directed. "Let's see where some of those bayous lead."

"Okay," said Al. "But none of those little inlets reaches to the ocean or ever has so long as I've been around here—and that's all my life!"

A closer view appeared to upset a theory Frank had that at one time there might have been a channel leading to a harbor. But now every finger of water was choked by stumps or ended in a mass of vegetation.

The amphibian spiraled slowly upward again, then made another run over the area.

"Say," Frank cried out suddenly, "the pond does have a big loop in it directly in the center of the ocean side, and one of these fingers runs straight toward the sea."

The others agreed. Then Frank added, "I see something else. That finger of water is of a lighter shade than the pond. There may still be an underground stream running from the ocean to the pond—but not enough to cause any perceptible rise and fall of the pond with the tide."

"Why is the inlet lighter?" Joe asked.

"Probably a different kind of soil underneath," remarked Al. "Well, fellows, do you all want to head back now?"

"Hold it!" Joe cried suddenly. "There's a boat! On one of those strips of water!"

Al kicked his ship into a sharp wing over that brought his craft low over the spot. A rowboat was quickly pulled out of sight in the hanging moss.

"What would a boat be doing in there?" Frank wondered.

"Yes," Joe put in. "I'd like to go down and find that man!"

"Maybe we can," Frank suggested. "How about it, Al? Could you set us down on the pond?"

Apprehensively the pilot checked the clouded skies. He looked at his watch.

"Okay," he agreed. "But don't make it long. When that storm hits, she'll be a honey. I want this ship safe in her hangar long before then!"

Veering round, the silver craft came in just over the cypresses, glided onto the pond, and floated toward shore.

Quickly the Hardys rigged mooring lines. Then the brothers waded ashore and plunged into the swamp.

Ducking under vines and hanging moss, leaping from one solid foothold to another, they pushed toward the spot where they had seen the rowboat disappear.

Under the cypresses, silence prevailed. In spite of the unsettled weather above, the thick mossy curtains scarcely moved. Frank and Joe forged ahead and presently found themselves beside a wide stream, which was running toward the pond.

Frank tasted the water. "Fresh," he announced.

Narrowing and branching, the little stream led them deeper into the treacherous area. At last Joe halted, crouching, behind a huge fallen tree trunk. Ahead, through the moss, he had spotted the rowboat.

A blue-shirted, slightly built man with his back to the boys leaned over the stern. He wore gloves. Hand over hand, he brought up a dripping object in a net.

"A baby alligator!" Frank whispered.

The man dropped the reptile into a deep box on his boat, and lowered his net again. Twice more the Hardys watched him bring up a similar catch.

"That's illegal," Frank commented quietly. He slipped over the huge tree trunk and crept ahead. Joe, following, supported himself against one of the tree's low-hanging limbs. Suddenly the branch gave way with a loud *crack*.

Instantly the stranger dropped low in his boat.

The next moment he came up again with a blue shotgun barrel trained in the Hardys' direction. A blast and a puff of gray smoke followed rapidly. Deadly pellets ripped shreds in the hanging moss and leaves just beside the brothers.

Frank and Joe were hugging the mucky earth when the second blast sounded. This time the shot rattled into a fallen tree trunk right behind them.

"Keep down!" Frank warned. "He may have another shell ready!"

But now the stranger was bending low over his oars. With quick pulls on them he sent the boat up the little stream, and in a moment was out of sight around a bend.

"Better let him go if we don't want to get shot," Frank said. "Let's look at the alligator nest."

Frank and Joe clambered forward to the mudbank.

"Besides poaching baby alligators," said Frank, "he was stealing the eggs, too. Look. There's the nest he was rifling."

The boy pointed to a freshly dug mound of mud at the very end of the oozy bank. Half sunk in the muck and water was a fallen tree trunk. Balancing themselves, the boys walked out on it for a look.

"I guess these poachers sell the baby alligators to tourists and pet shops," Joe said.

"Well, the fellow should be reported," Frank

stated flatly. "Alligators in this country are protected by law against poaching. That's why he shot at us."

Stooping, Frank peered into the muddy hole, but no eggs were visible. He straightened up, then looked around, puzzled.

"Say, which way is the plane? We couldn't have come far, but I've lost my sense of direction in this place."

"Yell," Joe suggested. "When Al answers, we'll know which way to go."

"*Al! Al West!*" The boys' voices echoed through the silent swamp.

"Louder!" Joe urged, cupping his hands and taking in a tremendous breath. "*Hey—Al! Where are you?*"

In his strenuous effort, the boy lost his balance on the slippery trunk. With a splash he went down into the water. Grabbing the trunk with both hands, he tried to hoist himself out.

"My legs! They're caught in some vines!" he gasped.

Stooping to aid his brother, Frank spotted a sudden movement on the surface of the stream. Then he recognized the snout of an alligator. The angry reptile was swimming straight toward Joe!

CHAPTER XIII

Hurricane

JOE, trapped, blanched when he caught sight of the oncoming alligator. Frank balanced himself on the fallen trunk and glanced quickly about for a means of rescue. A stout log about four feet long floated by. Seizing the log, Frank lifted it over his head in both hands.

When the alligator's ugly snout came into range, Frank hurled his weapon with a mighty thrust. A solid crack told him that the heavy log had struck the animal's head. The huge reptile rolled over, its short legs flailing helplessly and tail lashing from side to side.

Meanwhile, Frank jumped into the water beside his brother. Three quick slashes with his jack-knife severed the underwater vines, and the two boys scrambled onto the trunk in safety.

"Whew!" Joe gulped. "Thanks, lifesaver! Let's go."

The brothers once more started off in the direction they judged the seaplane to be. "Al!" they kept shouting. "Al West!"

No answer from the pilot came through the dim swamp. But now, the tops of the cypresses swayed and the hanging moss quivered as the advance winds of the storm began to pick up. Suddenly, from some distance behind the Hardys, an airplane engine roared.

"We've been heading in the wrong direction!" Frank cried out. "Come on! Hurry!"

The treacherous, boggy ground prevented quick progress, however. All around the light was quickly dimming. Frank and Joe forged doggedly on, and finally the throb of the plane's engine grew louder.

"We're getting there!" Frank panted in relief.

At last they broke through to the shore of the pond. Overhead, dark shreds of clouds were being driven across the sky like streams of smoke. A light rain slanted across the water and Al West, with a worried frown, was just about to take off.

Upon seeing Frank and Joe, he gave a joyful shout. "You were gone such a long time," he called, "I got scared, and revved up the motor for a signal. Storm's arriving ahead of schedule. If we take off now, we'll just about make it!"

Quickly the boys climbed aboard. Turning the

plane, Al ran it down the pond until she rose, bucking, into the stiff gusts of the approaching storm.

Now the lead-gray sea, crossed with white foam, was running high up the beach below.

"Chet!" Frank exclaimed suddenly. "He's had no warning of the hurricane. We must get to him. Al, can you set us down near our camp?"

The pilot looked out his window, against which the rain was beating hard. "Sea's getting too mean for this ship," he said. "Even that fishing smack has run for shelter somewhere. I know! There's a flat, firm beach a little way up from your place."

Minutes later, the skilled pilot brought his plane down in a neat landing only yards from the big breakers now crashing higher and higher up the sand.

"So long—good luck!" the Hardys called as Al lifted his craft into the buffeting air currents once more, and winged for the airport.

Frank and Joe plowed through the sand toward camp. "Wow!" Joe exclaimed, struggling against the wind. "It must be blowing at forty miles an hour already!"

Whirling sand and gale-driven rain slashed at the boys as they raced along the beach and rounded the big dune. Just as they did, Frank gave a shout.

"Our tent!"

Their canvas shelter, straining from its one remaining rope, suddenly jerked loose and was carried off by the howling wind.

Fearfully the brothers looked around the devastated camp, now a confusion of ropes, poles, and blowing sand. There was no sign of Chet.

"Maybe he's taken shelter," Joe yelled above the screaming gale. "We'd better find some ourselves!"

"Let's try the underground passage to Rand's," Frank decided quickly. "It's the safest place."

As the winds increased to hurricane force, making a continual eerie wail in the scrubby pines, the boys set out on a loping run from the beach toward the pond.

The storm rose to full fury. The sky had become pitch dark, although it was only about six o'clock. Cold, heavy sheets of rain drove in sideways from the sea. The wind pressed relentlessly at the boys' backs.

They were forced to break into a fast run along the pond toward Rand's. Suddenly, above them, came an explosive splintering sound.

"Look out!" Frank yelled, yanking Joe aside.

The next instant an enormous dead oak, throwing up its network of roots, landed right in front of the boys!

"Close call!" cried Joe.

They skirted around the fallen tree, and pounded uphill toward the hedge. Then they rolled down the steep embankment on the other

The winds increased to hurricane force

side, and groped their way until they found the heavy wooden door. At last, exhausted, they stumbled into the dry darkness of the old brick passage.

The sound of voices and a flickering light came from the old beverage room ahead. As the Hardys dashed in, a bulky, comical-looking person was taking off hat after hat, coat after coat, blanket after blanket, shirt after shirt. Looking on and laughing were Grover and his grandson Timmy.

"Chet Morton!" Frank cried with mingled relief and amusement. "Clowning it up in the middle of a hurricane!"

Their friend turned his grinning face to them. "Had to do something to keep from worrying about you fellows. Thank goodness you're okay!"

Then he explained cheerfully, "Couldn't waste time carrying clothes. Had more important things to carry." Chet pointed to a well-packed carton of groceries. "So I just wore everything I could."

"Why didn't you wear the tent, too?" Joe needled. "We just saw it blow away!"

Chet had rescued enough shirts and trousers for Frank and Joe to change into dry clothing.

"Guess you all could use a bite to eat," said Grover. Immediately Chet went into action. The stout boy dug into his supplies, and using Grover's little stove, soon had a steaming supper of stew, bread, and hot coffee for everyone.

Afterward, the five drew chairs up to the

wooden table and listened to the shrieking of the wind outside.

"Man, that's some storm!" Chet commented.

"Yes, sir, it sure is," Grover agreed. "But I reckon it's not so bad as the one grandpappy used to tell about when I was just a mite of a boy. That big storm came when *he* was a young fellow, just after the Civil War. Waves were as big as houses, he said. Knocked down so many trees and blew things so every which way, nobody could recognize this place after it was over!"

"It must have been the same blow we read about this morning in the old town newspapers," Frank said.

The old man took a thoughtful look at his ceiling. "Yes, sir," he went on, "that old storm did such a powerful lot of damage, it was all folks could do to straighten things out."

While Grover went on to tell of other bad storms, little Timmy listened with wide eyes. Now and then he fingered some little trinket from his pocket.

"What have you there, Timmy?" Joe asked curiously. "May I see it?"

Shyly the boy lowered his eyes and shook his head.

"Come on," Joe coaxed. "I won't hurt it, cross my heart."

But the youngster retreated behind his grandfather and plunged both hands into his pockets.

"I have an idea," said Frank in a short time. "Let's play a game. Each person has to take two things he doesn't especially want out of his pocket, and put them on the table. He must tell where he got them. Afterward, each player chooses one thing from somebody else and keeps it."

Chet and Joe exchanged comprehending glances with Frank. "Here's a chocolate bar and a lucky rabbit's foot," said the stout boy. "I bought the candy and the rabbit's foot at a stationer's."

Soon the wooden table was covered with small articles. Timmy, eying them excitedly, laid out a chipped arrowhead and a flat stone blade.

"That's a hide scraper," Frank thought excitedly. "An Indian one!"

"Found 'em in the dirt," Timmy said hurriedly, "near the pond by a big old dead oak."

"Okay, Timmy," said Frank, trying to conceal his excitement. "You're sure you want to part with these?"

"Oh, yes, sir."

"Okay. Now you choose something you'd like."

Eagerly the little boy snatched up a flashlight key chain that Joe had put down. Joe picked up the chipped arrowhead and Frank chose the hide scraper. The boys offered the rest of the items to Timmy, who scooped them up happily.

Later, Chet, sensing that the Hardys wanted to

examine their "winnings," encouraged Grover to reminisce some more about local events.

Frank and Joe bent over the artifacts. "These must be from the lost Indian village Professor Rand is looking for," Joe surmised.

Frank agreed. "If we could only find the actual site," he said, "maybe we could bargain with Rand. We'll trade him relics for information about the Blackstone family."

The storm continued unabated. As the night wore on, old Grover and Timmy lay down on cots at the back of the beverage room. Frank, Joe, and Chet, not sleepy, sat up around the kerosene lamp and talked in low voices. At last the sound of the wind dropped off, and finally stopped altogether.

"Must be about over," said Joe. He checked his watch. "It's almost morning."

Leaving the old man and the boy asleep, the three blew out the lamp and slipped into the passage. Cautiously they pushed open the heavy door and emerged into the meadow.

A light rain still fell, with short gusts of wind. But overhead, the first light of dawn was showing in the gray-white sky.

"The worst is past," Frank announced. "It'll clear off later."

The boys made their way with difficulty toward the pond. Enormous uprooted trees lay on the ground, some crisscrossed atop one another. Logs and leafy debris floated on the surface of the pond.

The boys headed for the beach. Even from a distance they could see huge waves still running up much farther than usual.

"Where's our campsite?" Chet gasped. "And the two big dunes?"

A completely flat beach lay around them for hundreds of yards.

"Vanished!" declared Frank, astounded. "You'd never know they'd been here!"

Suddenly his own words seemed to electrify the youth. Frank whirled and began to run. "Back to the pond," he called to the others.

Mystified, Joe and Chet raced after him. Soon, breathing hard, they gazed again on a completely changed scene of fallen trees, uprooted brush, and new pools of water. Portions of the bank had been broken down and washed into the pond.

"Yes, of course!" Frank exclaimed. "This is it!"

Joe's eyes lit up with excitement as he, too, suddenly understood.

"Is what?" Chet asked blankly.

"Hidden Harbor!" Frank exulted. "We've found it!"

CHAPTER XIV

A Revealing Argument

"We've found Hidden Harbor?" asked Chet, eagerly looking around. "Where is it?"

"Right here!" Frank answered jubilantly. "The pond *is* Hidden Harbor!"

The stout boy appeared more puzzled than ever.

"It just occurred to me," Frank explained, "if the hurricane we had last night could wipe out those big sand dunes and knock over trees the size of these around here, what a terrific amount of damage the tremendous Civil War storm must have caused. It could have changed the topography around this whole bay! Probably closed up the channel from the ocean with silt, trees, brush, and sand. If pirates did use Hidden Harbor, they had to stop their smuggling into it."

Excitedly Joe snapped his fingers. "Remember the wide strip of lighter water we spotted from the air? That's part of the old channel! After the Civil War hurricane it became clogged with sand."

"Whoopee!" Chet cried, elated at the discovery. "When do we start looking for the buried fortune? Grover said it's at the mouth of the harbor. That would be the side of the pond nearest the ocean."

"Yes," Frank confirmed. "We start right away. But first we'll need our skin-diving equipment."

"I hope there's something left of it," Joe said gloomily.

"Oh, I put the gear in the trunk of the car," Frank reminded him. "It ought to be all right. Say! Where *is* the car, Chet?"

"Parked in some pines a few hundred yards from the beach."

"I'll bring back the equipment," Frank offered. "Meantime, why don't you two take a half hour's rest? I'll see you at the pond."

Accordingly, Frank hiked to the pine trees alone. He found the yellow convertible undamaged, but half covered by drifting sand. Frank cleared the car, and took out the diving gear. It was intact. He hoisted the rucksack containing the outfits to his shoulders and headed for the pond.

As he neared it, Frank passed the huge fallen oak. He looked about for Chet and Joe. He was about to call out when the sound of an angry voice made him duck behind an old gnarled tree. The harsh tones were those of Samuel Blackstone!

With a crash of brush the heavy-set man broke into the open space in front of Frank's hiding place. Behind him trailed the beanpole figure of Henry Cutter.

"No!" roared Blackstone. "I positively will *not* sell my rights to this pond. Can't you get that through your head, Cutter?"

"You'll have to admit, though, the pond has been nothing but trouble to you," Cutter said unctuously. "Indirectly, it has damaged your family name, and led you into bringing a lawsuit. Why, it's even caused you to reopen the old family quarrel with Rand. What good *is* it to you?"

"And what use is it to *you,* sir, may I ask?" Blackstone retorted.

"Mr. Stewart and I," Cutter said patiently, "as I've told you, would like to purchase this water, with the surrounding land, to set up a small private fishing club. We would stock the pond, open a channel to the ocean, and bring parties in by motorboat."

"Fishing club!" snorted Blackstone. "Do you think I was born yesterday, Cutter? What's your real game? You're in with Rand, aren't you? The two of you—trying to get my property. That intellectual thinks he knows where to find the lost fortune, and wants it for himself!"

Infuriated, Blackstone seized his pale companion and shook him.

"No one is getting a square inch of my land or a drop of this pond while I'm alive!" he thundered. "You hear? Not while I'm alive!"

With that, he released the thinner man and strode off. Cutter, paler than ever, glared after the retreating Blackstone. Then he turned abruptly and disappeared into the swamp.

"Wish I had time to follow Cutter," Frank thought. "But right now I have another job."

After waiting a few minutes, Frank emerged from behind the tree. A familiar low whistle came from above. He looked up. Peering at him from a strong tree limb, sat Joe and Chet! Quickly the two boys dropped to the ground.

"We heard Blackstone shouting," Joe told his brother, "so we shinned up out of sight."

"Saw the whole thing," Chet added.

"Some hot argument!" Joe remarked. "Seems to prove Cutter isn't working for Blackstone. Do you make anything else out of it?"

"Only this," Frank replied. "The old feud was caused by both the Blackstones' and the Rands' knowing about Clement's buried treasure. The feud started not just because of the division of land, but because each side thought the treasure was buried somewhere between those two oak trees, and wouldn't give up one foot of ground."

Chet sighed. "Boy, this thing's sure getting

complicated. Well, are you ready to go diving?"

"Ready."

Chet helped Frank and Joe put on their diving equipment.

"This will be the first time we've been down in daylight," Frank noted. "Visibility ought to be a lot better."

"You'd better take your spears in with you," Chet warned, "in case that monster is lurking underwater!"

Soon the boys submerged off the ocean side of the pond. The sun had broken through, and Chet, straining his eyes, could see the boys kicking along with their flippers, testing the bottom. But finally they moved off into deeper water.

For two hours the search went on. The swimmers dug into mud and sand, and poked their spearheads into caverns formed by twisting cypress roots. Occasionally, they surfaced to rest.

During one of their pauses, Frank said, "The money and papers are probably in a metal chest. Hard to guess the size, since we don't know how much is in it."

"A tremendous amount of silt could have settled over it since the stuff was buried," Joe remarked.

The brothers continued the underwater search but were unable to find any metal object.

"There's a mess of sand down there," said Joe as the divers removed their gear. "What we need are some real digging and scraping tools."

"Yes, and a metal detector," Frank added. "We ought to be able to pick up one in Larchmont."

"We'll go shopping later," Frank said, "if we can get our car started."

"Why don't we go right away, fellows?" Chet complained. "We haven't eaten in ages. I'm all hollow inside."

"Why, Chet!" Joe grinned, fully dressed once more. "Who wants to eat when we can spend profitable hours looking for Indian relics?"

"Relics," Chet lamented. "You can't eat a relic."

Joe took the arrowhead from his pocket and examined it. "Timmy says he found it right near the dead oak at the left of the pond," he said.

"Sounds logical," Frank reasoned. "The tree probably stood there for a couple of centuries. If there ever *was* an Indian village in this spot, it might have been a favorite place for the men to sit and chip arrowheads."

"I'd like to chip my teeth on a nice big steak!" muttered Chet.

Frank took pity on their suffering friend. "We're hungry, too. We'll eat soon, honest. But as long as we're here, let's dig around the tree."

"All right!" Chet sighed. "But you still haven't any tools."

"We won't need tools," Frank assured him. "The hurricane's done our digging for us."

He led the way along the pond toward the Rand property to the upper branches of the fallen oak. They followed the enormous trunk to the huge round hole in the earth, where the tree had stood. The pit, nearly five feet deep at the center, yawned open in front of them.

Stepping down into it, the boys began to sift the still-damp earth through their fingers.

"Found something!" Joe called after a few minutes. "Thin and flat, like a dime."

"It's a bird point," Frank announced after a brief examination. "A small, fine arrowhead for killing birds.

"We're getting somewhere, all right," Frank said cheerfully. As he shifted his position in the pit, his canvas sneaker seemed to catch on something solid. Stooping, he loosened and drew out the muddy fragment of a curved surface.

"Pottery!" he exclaimed. "Here's another piece. There seems to be more stuff at this lower level!"

Working swiftly, the boys unearthed several more large pieces of old clay vessels. In addition, Joe found a wedge-shaped stone that might have been used as an axhead.

He straightened up suddenly. "Fellows, I think we've found the site of the ancient Indian village!"

CHAPTER XV

Sea City Hoax

THE HARDYS and Chet felt a thrill of discovery. "So this is the lost Indian village!" Frank said as the three climbed from the relic-filled depression.

"Now," said Joe, "we'll have something to offer Professor Rand in exchange for information."

"Yes," Frank agreed. "Also, Rand, or a trained archaeologist, will consider our find more valuable if it's relatively undisturbed. We'll take these arrowheads and pottery shards as proof we've found the site."

The boys carefully covered over the place they had dug up. After cleaning the relics in the pond, Frank asked Chet to get a bag or carton from Grover in which to carry them.

"If it means we're heading for town—and food," the hungry boy said, "I'll do it."

When Chet returned with a carton, they packed

it and started back for the beach. Chet and Joe carried the diving gear while Frank clutched the precious relics.

They reached the yellow convertible and Frank opened the door to place the carton on the rear floor. He groaned. "There's a ton of sand in here!"

The hard-driven sand had filtered into the vehicle and piled up regular mounds on the seats and floor!

"Hope the engine isn't full of sand, too," Joe said, after the boys had cleaned out the interior. He took the wheel and tried to start the car. Nothing happened.

The mechanically minded Hardys wasted no time in getting the hood raised. Joe cleaned and wiped the spark plugs, then checked the wiring for short circuits. Meantime, Frank and Chet, drawing some gasoline from the tank, bathed the parts which had become clogged by the driving sand.

Soon the pistons were operating smoothly. Slipping into low gear, Joe gunned the engine. With Frank and Chet pushing, the convertible plowed steadily through the drifted sand to the road.

"We'd better report to Bart Worth first thing," said Frank.

They found Larchmont in the midst of mopping up after the hurricane. Power-line crews were busy, and throughout the town fallen trees were being cut up with roaring power saws, and hauled away.

The boys parked and went up to the offices of the *Larchmont Record*. "What a madhouse!" Chet exclaimed.

The place was filled with the din of clacking typewriters and typesetting machines, jangling telephones, and shouting between copy-desk editors and reporters. Printers with ink-smeared aprons rushed in and out of the composing room. Bart Worth, looking exhausted, moved about in shirt sleeves giving directions.

He hailed the Hardys and Chet with a shout of relief and hustled them into his private office. "I was sure worried about you fellows. Hope you found shelter. We've been busy all night covering this storm."

"We made out okay," Joe assured him.

"Good." Bart gave a weary sigh and began pacing the floor. "I have more trouble. Blackstone's used his influence with the court, and had the trial moved up! If I don't get proof soon, I'm sunk."

"We may have some helpful news for you," Frank announced quietly. "In the first place, *we're* convinced that the smuggling story is true."

He and Joe went on to give a full account of their experiences and discoveries since they had last seen Bart.

The editor's eyes brightened with amazement and hope. "So," he said, "the Rand-Blackstone pond was once a secret harbor, connected to the sea by a channel! What a perfect setup for the Blackstones to conduct their smuggling operations."

Then Bart Worth's face clouded. "But how can we prove all this?"

"By finding the family papers," Frank replied. "They're buried at the mouth of the old Hidden Harbor. The only problem is," the boy admitted, "how to locate *that*."

At this point Joe held up the box of ancient Indian artifacts.

"We'll try to set up a trade with Professor Rand," he explained, "by telling him where to find the Indian village, providing he'll tell us where to find the proof we need—if he knows."

Bart nodded. "It's the way to Ruel Rand's heart, all right," he agreed. "But can you catch up with him in time?"

"We'll do our best," Frank promised.

"Say! I have another lead," the editor burst out suddenly. "Almost forgot with this hurricane business. This morning I received a call from a man who claimed to be Jenny Shringle's cousin in Sea City. According to him, Jenny has changed her mind—wants to tell me something important about the case. I'm supposed to meet her late this afternoon in the lobby of the Surfside Hotel in

Sea City, and bring you fellows with me."

"Sounds phony to me!" was Joe's prompt reaction. "A convenient way to get us all in one place, then get rid of us!"

"Still, it *may* be a real lead," the editor insisted. "We can't afford to pass it up."

"Then why the secrecy?" Joe demanded. "And why does she want Frank and me along?"

"She may be afraid of Blackstone," Worth argued. "Besides, I think she's grateful to you boys for rescuing her in the fun house."

"We'll go, then," Frank assented, "but I wouldn't be too hopeful about it, Bart."

While Bart Worth toiled feverishly to get his hurricane edition on the presses, the three hungry friends went to a restaurant which Chet Morton had selected well in advance. After a hearty steak and dessert of fresh peach shortcake, Chet revived noticeably.

"One little thing bothers me," he said. "We don't have a camp any more. No tent, no food. Our clothes and blankets are at Grover's hideout, and most of our utensils were buried in the sand. Besides," he added, "you fellows need digging tools and a metal detector."

"In other words," Frank said, laughing, "you're volunteering to stay here, buy what we need, and set up camp again."

"You've guessed it!" Chet admitted. "I'm more sure of regular meals and sleep, too."

Soon the trio separated, and Chet took the yellow convertible to do his errands. A little later Frank, Joe, and Bart Worth set out for Sea City in the editor's green sedan. Clouds had covered the sun again, and gusts of wind shook the car as it sped along the highway.

"We're early," Frank noted. "We may as well pick up Jenny at her cousin's, Bart."

The three went up and knocked at the little white bungalow. The same middle-aged man they had met previously opened the door.

"We've come about your phone call this morning, Mr. Shringle," Bart explained.

"Phone call?" the man repeated, bewildered. "Jenny! Did you telephone and ask these folks to come here?"

Now the short, plump woman appeared at her cousin's side. She peered at the visitors suspiciously.

"I told you all once—I'm not allowed to talk to you," Jenny said.

The Hardys and Bart Worth exchanged meaningful glances. The phone call *had* been a hoax!

Frank turned to the seamstress. "Sorry to have bothered you, Miss Shringle. Guess it was a mix-up."

When the three returned to the car, Joe urged, "Let's go to the hotel, anyway. Maybe we can turn the tables and nab the gang we told you we heard on the fishing boat."

The others agreed and soon Bart parked near a long, two-story wooden building that was badly in need of fresh paint. Old-fashioned, high-backed rocking chairs, mostly empty, were distributed along a front porch which was as wide as the old hotel itself.

"Bart, you go up on the porch and wait," Frank proposed, "Joe and I will circle the place to see if anybody's lurking outside."

Quickly the Hardys moved around the run-down hotel. In the rear were several wings, also with porches, looking toward the beach. No one was in sight.

"Must have been quite a place in its heyday," Joe observed. "Sure is dead now, though."

The brothers returned to the porch to look for Bart Worth. But the editor was not in sight. A bald old man, seated in a rocking chair next to the main entrance, eyed them with open curiosity.

"Maybe Bart went back to the car," Joe suggested. "I'll check." He soon came back, shaking his head.

"Let's go into the lobby," Frank said.

Perplexed, the two boys walked into the dark shabby foyer, with its worn carpets. A curtain of hanging strands of bright-colored beads covered a doorway at the back of a hall next to a stairway. The place seemed empty; even the room clerk's desk was deserted. Frank and Joe strolled out to the porch, where the bald man in the rocking chair stared at them once more.

"Was there a man with reddish hair waiting here when you sat down?" Joe asked him.

The elderly man did not answer immediately and continued to gawk at the boys. Finally he drawled, "Yes. One was standing here. Bellman came out—said the stranger had a phone call. Must still be talkin', I reckon."

"Where's the phone?" Joe asked quickly.

"Go though the hangin' curtain," the man directed. "Phone's in the corridor there—right beside the back stairs."

"Bart must have walked right into the snare!" Frank whispered worriedly as the brothers stepped to the entrance.

Suddenly Joe grasped Frank's arm and pointed into the dim lobby. A man had appeared behind the reservations desk. The boys recognized him instantly: Mr. Stewart, Henry Cutter's partner. Now Stewart leaned across the counter to talk to a uniformed bellman.

"What's *he* doing here?" Joe muttered. "Working? Antique business must be bad."

The next moment, to the boys' surprise, the bellman came striding out to the porch.

"Frank and Joe Hardy?" he asked them. "Telephone call for you in the back hall. It's by the stairs."

CHAPTER XVI

Enemy Tactics

QUICK as a flash Frank decided on a plan of action. "I'll take the call," he told the bellman.

As the employee walked off, Frank murmured to Joe, "If it's a trap, I'll chance it alone. You stay free in case I need help."

"Okay. I'll go up the main staircase in the lobby," Joe volunteered, "and look for the back steps next to the phone."

Re-entering the lobby, the boys noted that the room clerk's desk was vacant once more. Joe climbed the wide stairway, while Frank ducked through the curtain of hanging beads.

He found himself in a dim hallway lighted only by a tiny window at the end. Near the rear, Frank spotted an old-time wall telephone, with the receiver dangling almost to the floor. Warily, he approached it.

Frank noted that all the room doors were closed except one just across from the phone. This was slightly ajar. Watching the door carefully, he reached the telephone. Frank stood listening intently. The old hotel was almost unnaturally quiet. Suddenly the young sleuth stiffened. From behind the open door came the familiar sound of hoarse, wheezy breathing!

"Jed!" Frank thought.

Deliberately, the boy turned his back. At the same time, he grasped the telephone cord in his right hand.

His straining ears caught a footfall on the carpet. Whirling, Frank swung the heavy receiver by its cord and caught the flat-faced man a smashing blow on the ear. With a cry of pain, the angered thug lurched forward and seized Frank's right arm in an iron grip. Frank immediately sent three chopping left jabs into the fellow's midriff. Now another figure came racing down the dim hallway. Stewart!

"Got him!" he cried, reaching Frank and pinning the boy's arm behind his back.

At the same instant there was a screeching whoop from above! Both assailants' heads jerked upward. Joe Hardy had vaulted onto the backstairs banister, and slid down full speed, crashing feet first against the burly man's chest. Frank wrenched free and landed a stiff uppercut on Stewart's jaw. The two boys bounded up the staircase and along the second-floor corridor.

"Here!" cried Joe, ducking into an open, vacant room. From the staircase came the pounding steps of their pursuers. Then the boys heard the opening and slamming of doors along the hall.

Passing from one suite to another through connecting doors, the boys dodged their enemy. When the chase was over, and it was quiet in the corridor, they cautiously tiptoed outside.

The next instant Joe cocked his head. "I'm sure I hear groans—in here!"

He yanked open the door to a large linen closet. Bart Worth, bound and gagged, lay on the floor. Quickly Frank and Joe released him. Overhead, the ceiling shook under heavy running footsteps up and down the third floor.

"Good! Those crooks are looking for us upstairs!" Joe said.

But before the trio could slip out of the hotel, they heard Stewart and Jed dashing downstairs. Pulling the closet door shut, the three friends lay low while the men rushed past and down to the lobby.

Frank, Joe, and Bart stepped into the hall. Frank, carrying a large hamper of clean linen, went to the second-floor landing and looked around. The floor boards creaked loudly beneath him.

"There they are!" cried Stewart from the foot of the stairs.

As the thugs, followed by the bellman, charged up the wide staircase again, Frank suddenly heaved the big hamper at them. A blizzard of white sheets, towels, and pillowcases billowed down upon the men. While they struggled to disentangle themselves, Bart cried, "Leave them alone. We'll get the police!"

He and the boys sprinted for the front door. They ran to Bart's car and roared away from the old hotel.

"Sorry to get myself caught like that," the editor apologized. "But I'd told my office to reach me here if I received an important phone call I've been expecting. So I really fell for it, when the bellman paged me."

"Who jumped you?" Joe asked. "Stewart and his crony Jed?"

"Yes. I heard them talk about somebody they called 'the boss,' who wanted the 'three troublemakers gotten rid of this time without fail!' "

"We were sure Blackstone wasn't behind this scheme," Joe remarked. "Now, I don't know what to believe, after that faked call from Jenny Shringle."

By this time Bart had pulled up at the Sea City police headquarters. Inside, the editor reported the assault on himself and the boys. Two squad cars were dispatched with sirens screaming. The chief asked the Hardys and Bart to remain in case they should be needed to identify their assailants.

Frank and Joe, however, felt sure that Stewart and Jed had already left the hotel. Their conclusion proved to be correct. When the officers returned, they reported that the thugs and the bellman, whom the men evidently had bribed, had fled. The manager, who doubled as clerk, had been away during the fracas.

"We'll find those hoods!" Frank declared as Bart and the Hardys drove off. "They can't get away with this!"

Bart said he would treat the Hardys to supper in Larchmont. As they ate, the brothers tried to cheer the young editor, who appeared greatly depressed.

"I'll bet Blackstone *was* behind this ambush," Bart insisted. "He'd be most apt to use Jenny Shringle's name. But I can't prove that, either!"

"Somehow I doubt he'd go to such lengths to win a libel suit," Frank stated. "Even if his family's reputation is at stake. Don't forget," he reasoned, *"Cutter's* men worked this trap. We did overhear Cutter in a real argument with Blackstone this morning. Of course, they could be working together to get rid of us, and still fighting among themselves."

"In any case, the three of us are in real danger," Bart stated grimly.

"Yes, the three of us," cried Frank, rising suddenly from the table, "and Chet! He's all alone!

Those hoods know we'd do anything to rescue Chet if they kidnaped him!"

Hastily Bart paid the check and they ran to the car. All maintained an anxious silence as they sped for Larchmont. At last the sedan was on the fishermen's road, heading for the campsite.

When they reached it, Frank, Joe, and the editor leaped from the car and turned on flashlights. A scene of devastation such as that caused by the hurricane met their eyes. Food, clothing, equipment lay strewn around. A brand-new tent slashed in ribbons hung from its pole. In the sand was a confusion of footprints.

"We're too late!" Joe groaned. "Chet's gone!"

Suddenly, on the shore road, two yellow headlights approached the stunned trio.

"They're coming back!" Frank said.

Quickly the three put out their lights and ducked behind a clump of small pines. The car drew up and stopped. The door slammed. Someone shuffled across the sand. An unmistakable tuneless whistle warbled on the night air.

"Chet!"

Frank, Joe, and Bart rushed forward in joyful relief to greet their friend.

"Sure it's me," replied the stout boy. "Who else? Hey!" He clapped a hand to his head. "Leapin' lizards! What went through this place? The new tent ruined! My pots and pans! My food!"

"Don't worry about it," Frank said. "The main thing is, you're okay. Where *did* you go?"

"Got lonesome and went to the movies. I'm sorry, fellows. Guess I'm a punk guard."

"You did the right thing," Frank assured him. "You wouldn't have stood a chance against those crooks! They wrecked this place."

The boys then told their friend of the Sea City adventure.

Chet gulped. "I sure *was* lucky. We can always get a new tent—and more food!"

Everyone laughed, including Bart, whose spirits seemed to have lifted. Some minutes later, the editor said good night.

As the taillights of Bart's car disappeared down the road, Chet and the Hardys set about restoring what order they could. Suddenly Joe called out, "Hey—a light! Way in the distance. Might be in the swamp around Rand's property!"

Immediately Frank ran over to his brother. "Maybe it's the tall fellow we think is the professor! Let's take the Indian relics and have a talk with him!"

Fortunately, the valued artifacts had been locked in the convertible's trunk. The boys lifted out the carton and set out. Soon, with flashlights off, they were treading carefully around the pond.

"Sh!" Frank warned the boys and stopped. "I thought I saw something move in the swamp!"

The searchers peered intently ahead. Everything appeared motionless. Again they went forward. Out of nowhere, it seemed, a gleam of light darted about in the swamp just ahead. As the boys crept steadily closer, they made out a familiar hat.

"Must be Rand!" Joe hissed. "He's examining something in his hand."

Wordlessly Frank motioned Joe to move up on one side of the man, and Chet the other. The boys set themselves to surround him in hopes of preventing a sudden flight.

"Help—help!"

A strangled cry followed by a heavy splash came from the dark pond behind them!

The long-coated man straightened up and started forward. But he stopped when the three boys broke from cover and dashed toward the pond in the direction of the cry. Now a child's terrified scream rent the night air.

Joe, in the lead, reached the bank of the pond first, and beamed his flashlight full ahead. To his astonishment, Grover and little Timmy were running back and forth, wailing and looking in panic toward the water.

"Quick, quick!" cried Timmy as Joe came up. "Some devil just pulled Mr. Blackstone under the water!"

CHAPTER XVII

Underwater Prison

"WHERE did Mr. Blackstone go down?" cried Joe. At the same time, Frank and Chet crashed through the bushes onto the bank of the pond.

"Th-there!" Timmy pointed to a swirl in the dark water about twenty feet from shore.

Chet held two flashlights while the Hardys plunged in. They submerged and stroked downward. Joe, groping his way through the underwater darkness, suddenly grasped what felt like clothing.

He could barely make out the shape of a heavyset person. Samuel Blackstone! Seizing one of the big man's arms, Joe tried to push upward. But he could make no progress. Blackstone was being dragged deeper!

While Joe kept tugging, Frank spotted his brother, glided in, and grasped Blackstone about the waist. Suddenly the boy came in contact with something soft and slippery, that was tightly clamped around the victim's body and holding him down!

"The monster!" Frank thought.

With all his might he wrenched at the slimy form until its grip was loosened. Though it wriggled back threateningly, Joe pulled Mr. Blackstone free.

Their lungs bursting, the swimmers bore the unconscious man to the surface. Chet quickly waded in and helped haul all three to shore.

"Timmy," ordered his grandfather, "you run up to the house and bring back help. Git, now!"

Meanwhile, Frank loosened Mr. Blackstone's clothing and administered artificial respiration. Joe, Chet, and Grover worriedly looked on, watching for signs of life.

Finally, to everyone's vast relief, Mr. Blackstone gasped, sputtered, and began breathing.

"Easy, sir," Frank cautioned him. "Just lie still and rest."

Joe turned to the elderly servant. "Did you see what happened? Tell us everything."

"I was taking my walk, as I do every night, when me and Timmy met Mr. Blackstone on the path. He hurried to the edge of the pond like he saw something. Next thing we knew, he gave a yell, and something dragged him right into the water!"

Now the waiting group heard excited voices,

then a series of lights could be seen winding toward them through the brush.

In a moment three of Mr. Blackstone's servants, carrying flashes, blankets, and axes, and led by little Timmy, reached the bank.

"Quick! Cut two saplings," Frank directed.

When this was done, the Hardys and Chet constructed an improvised stretcher, and Blackstone was lifted onto it and carried up to his house.

"Rand," he muttered incoherently as the boys and Grover waited in his spacious bedroom for the family physician to arrive. "Rand—did it."

Frank, Joe, and Chet stared at one another in puzzlement. They listened as Blackstone rambled on, "Rand—sent note—meet him at pond—talk over our differences—Rand did it."

At that moment the doctor entered and hurried to the man's bedside. After a quick examination, he warned, "Mr. Blackstone mustn't talk or be questioned. I must ask you all to leave."

The boys and Grover filed out. Joe whispered, "But Professor Rand couldn't have been responsible! He wasn't near the pond."

"Grover," Frank asked, "where does Mr. Blackstone keep his mail? We'd like to see that note from Professor Rand he just mentioned. I assure you we're trying to *help* Mr. Blackstone."

"He might not like it if I do what you ask," the butler objected.

"We'll have to take that chance," Frank said.

The servant nodded and led them downstairs to the study where the Hardys had witnessed the quarrel between the cousins. Grover handed Frank a spindle of papers from the desk. On top was a hand-printed note signed, "Ruel."

"I'll keep this for evidence," the boy told Grover. "I'll write a receipt for it."

After doing this, the three boys hurried back to camp. There Frank drew Professor Rand's map from the glove compartment of the convertible, and compared the printing to that on the note.

"Not the same!" Joe explained. "The note's a fake! Whoever sent it probably thought forged printing wouldn't be detected. But on this map Rand uses a little flourish at the beginning of each word."

"We must find Rand," Frank said soberly. "He's innocent, but not in Blackstone's eyes."

The boys headed for the pond. Off in the swamp they noticed the solitary light still moving about.

Joe started forward, but Frank restrained him, saying, "No—leave him there. Follow me."

The boy led the way to the Rand property and into the underground passage. They then entered the beverage room and lighted the lamp. Frank took care to leave the door ajar.

"Now," he said, "we'll wait for the professor here. He'll probably come home this way."

Some time later the boys heard the door to the

passage creak open. Slow, weary footsteps came along the corridor. Abruptly, the steps stopped in front of the beverage room.

"He's seen the light!" Joe whispered.

The Hardys and Chet shrank back behind the door, which moved inward. A tall figure in a raincoat and a floppy hat stepped toward the table.

Quickly Frank pushed the door shut, and the boys stood against it.

"Wh-what!" The man whirled.

"Please sit down, Professor Rand," said Frank. "We're sorry to startle you, but it's very important that we have a talk with you."

The tall man sank into a chair. Recovering his composure somewhat, he exclaimed, "Talk with prowlers and intruders! Never!"

"You *are* Professor Rand?" Frank queried.

"Of course I am. Who are *you?* And why are you snooping around?"

Pleasantly Frank made introductions, and explained that the boys had been retained by Bart Worth. "He asked us to help him prove that a certain story printed in his newspaper about the old Blackstone family *was* the truth."

Rand nodded. "What has that to do with me?"

Joe replied, "Mr. Blackstone nearly drowned in the pond tonight. Somebody or something pulled him in, and he's blaming you!"

The professor looked shocked. "How terrible! I did not realize that cry I heard was Samuel's. I was about to see who it was when I spotted you boys going toward the pond." Rand added emphatically, "Samuel and I may be at odds, but *I* would not resort to such tactics."

"You may be in danger yourself from the same thing," Frank told Rand. "You and Mr. Blackstone both claim this pond and the land around it. We boys have a hunch your cousin's assailant may be a person who has a nefarious interest in this property."

The boys then told of someone's locking them in Rand's room. The professor's startled reaction convinced them he had not done it. "To think the scoundrel followed me in and out of the house," he said worriedly.

"His accomplice must have locked the closet door from the tunnel side," Frank added. "They probably planned to harm us later, and didn't expect us to escape!"

"It was a close shave!" Joe murmured.

"We believe the person is doing all he can to block us," Frank said. "As you know, Professor, we must prove that the Blackstone fortune was made originally by smuggling. We understand the bulk of it is buried at the mouth of a hidden harbor."

"Humph! It's true," Professor Rand broke in, "if that's what you want to know. The pond between our properties was old Clement's harbor."

"So we've learned. But we need proof," Frank

told him. "If you'll furnish some, we may be able to give you a start toward unearthing the Indian village you're looking for."

The scholar's eyes lighted with interest and surprise, although he asked dubiously, "How do I know you can do what you say?"

In answer, Frank handed over the professor's own map, while Joe held out the arrowhead and hide scraper.

This time Rand did not restrain his enthusiasm. "Wonderful! Perfect! Where were these found?"

"In a spot not far away from where we found plenty of other relics," Joe spoke up. "But we left most of them undisturbed."

There was a moment's silence while the professor weighed the offer. Finally he said, "I agree to the trade. And I'll carry out my end of the bargain first."

The Hardys and Chet listened eagerly as the professor went on. "I never had the slightest interest in the disputed property until I realized the area near the pond was probably the site of an old Indian village. Before excavating, I wanted a clear title to the land, and that started my quarrel with Samuel. He claimed I actually intended to dig for the buried fortune."

"Didn't you?" Joe asked.

"Not at first. But when nobody would underwrite the excavation, I decided I would *have* to find the treasure myself in order to finance it. Then, because I wanted no interference, and Samuel is so touchy about his family name, we agreed to cover up our disagreement. I 'disappeared' so I could hunt undisturbed for the money I hope to find."

"Both of you want the property for different reasons," Frank said. "Mr. Blackstone's mainly concerned about anyone else finding the treasure, because of the family papers concealed with it. Is our deduction right?"

Professor Rand nodded. "Exactly."

"Do *you* know where the fortune is, sir?" Joe asked suddenly.

"I've known it all my life, but it hasn't done me any good."

"Why not?" Chet burst out.

"I once read in a letter of my grandmother's that it was buried beneath a giant cypress at the mouth of the Hidden Harbor. The problem is, where *was* the cypress?"

For a moment, all four frowned in deep thought.

"I know!" Frank exulted.

Professor Rand, Joe, and Chet turned to him eagerly. "Tell us, pal!" Chet begged.

"Each time we've made a search of the pond, I've noticed a section of tangled root ends," Frank explained, "and, way underneath, a long irregular outline I knew was a huge fallen tree. That must have been the cypress which once stood beside the old channel at the harbor's mouth!"

"What are we waiting for?" Joe cried out.

The professor, as excited as the boys, hurried with them toward the beach. Soon the four, carrying tools, lights, diving equipment, and a metal detector, made their way eagerly back to the edge of the pond. Frank offered to dive first.

"Look out for the monster!" Joe warned.

Quickly Frank put on his outfit. He attached the lamp to his forehead and slung the metal detector at his belt. Then, taking a long-handled spade, he submerged.

Deeper and deeper Frank stroked. His lamp showed up the enormous fallen tree's mass of roots. Suddenly the detector began to click!

Frank swam under the huge roots and jabbed the spade into the silt. The steel tool thudded against something solid. Adjusting his lamp, Frank saw by its murky gleam what appeared to be the corner of a wooden chest.

"The treasure!" he thought elatedly. "The box is probably made of cypress wood to protect a metal chest!"

The object proved to be out of Frank's reach. Tough, gnarled roots well over a hundred years old had grown so closely around the chest that try as he might, Frank could not move it by hand or shovel.

Disappointed, he turned back through the tangle of roots. As Frank twisted in and out, his air line became fouled. It was tightly snagged between two roots! Frank struggled to free the line, but to no avail.

"Joe and the others expect me to stay down for a while," the trapped boy thought frantically. "Unless I can signal, they won't come after me until it's too late!"

CHAPTER XVIII

Dangerous Cargo

HOLDING his breath, Frank again fought desperately to free his air line from the binding roots. He thrashed his arms and legs in a futile effort to jerk it loose.

At last he worked one hand down to his lead-weighted belt, where his fingers tore open a small plastic compartment. From it he plucked a white ping-pong ball, which he sent bobbing through the roots toward the surface of the pond. This ball was a trouble signal the Hardy brothers had worked out.

"If only Joe's light picks it up!" Frank thought.

At the pond's edge, meanwhile, Joe, Chet, and Professor Rand watched the smooth surface.

"I'm actually going to see the long-lost family fortune," the professor declared. "I can hardly believe it!"

"Also," responded Joe, who stood by in his diving apparatus, "we'll have this case licked!"

Suddenly Chet exclaimed, "A white bubble!"

The next instant Joe spotted the ping-pong ball. "Frank's in danger!" he cried out and plunged underwater. He stroked down, his light beam piercing the dark water. As he approached the fantastically twisted cypress roots, Joe caught sight of Frank, struggling to free himself.

Joe drew his knife and moved in, cutting a path as he went. The two stout roots holding Frank gave way before the razor-sharp blade. Seizing his brother's limp arms, Joe maneuvered him through the roots to the surface.

For a moment the treasure was forgotten completely, while Chet and the professor worked to revive Frank. Luckily he had held his breath a long time, and had swallowed very little water. In a little while he was sitting up and being rubbed vigorously with a towel.

"I saw part of a chest," Frank told the others. "It's enmeshed in the silt and tree roots. We'll have to blast it out."

The boys suggested that they obtain dynamite and return the following day. Professor Rand agreed to the idea but reminded them that the next day was Sunday. "No stores will be open. We'll have to wait until Monday."

The group agreed to keep the matter a secret, then separated. The boys went back to their campsite, had a late snack, and bedded down on the sand under the open sky.

Monday morning was clear and sunshiny, as they headed for town in the yellow convertible.

First, Frank parked in front of a drugstore and went into the phone booth to call the Sea City police. In a few minutes he came back and reported, "They've had no luck tracking down those thugs who attacked us in the hotel."

The trio decided to enlist the editor's help in obtaining the dynamite. They went to his office and told of their discovery at the pond. Highly excited, Bart was glad to accompany the trio to make the purchase.

"Anything to retrieve that chest," he exclaimed as they entered Larchmont's only hardware store. Bart made his request to an elderly clerk.

"Dynamite, hey!" the shopkeeper repeated in a loud voice of surprise. Other customers turned to look. "One thing we don't have. Just a minute, though."

The clerk went to the cellar doorway and shouted down the stairs. "Henry! Folks here need some dynamite! Know where they can get some?"

Uneasily, the Hardys, Chet, and Bart glanced at the curious faces peering at them.

"What say?" came a voice from the cellar.

"*Dynamite*," roared the clerk. "Folks here want to do a little blasting!"

"Oh, *dynamite!*" Henry shouted back. "They can get it in Dobbsville!"

"Thanks very much," said Bart, and the four hastily left the store.

As they stepped into the car, Joe noted ruefully, "Well, if anyone in town doesn't know we need dynamite, they will in a few minutes!"

"You said it. Around here they don't need a loud-speaker!" Chet grinned.

Bart Worth directed the way to Dobbsville. Once there, he and the Hardys entered the hardware store, while Chet went off to make a purchase of his own. He returned with a paper bag just as the others were gingerly placing a small wooden case marked dynamite on the rear floor of the convertible.

"Dangerous cargo," Chet remarked.

"It sure is," Bart agreed, then asked the Hardys, "Do you fellows know how to handle this stuff?"

Frank nodded. "Dad has taught us about explosives."

"Right now," Chet put in, "let's eat!" Happily the stout boy pulled out some huge sandwiches filled with several layers of ham, lettuce, tomatoes, and cheese. "I got four of these for our lunch."

"Looks like a seven-course meal!" Joe teased.

Bart smiled. "I'd like to join you boys, but I have to do an errand, You go on ahead. I'll take a taxi back and meet you at the pond in an hour."

A few minutes later the Hardys and Chet were heading for Larchmont. The car crossed a crystal-clear brook winding through a shady stand of pines set back on a knoll.

"Stop!" ordered Chet. "Here's the place for our submarine sandwiches."

Laughing, the boys parked off the road and got out. Soon they were sprawled on the soft pine needle carpet of the grove, where they could just see the sunlight flashing on the front of the convertible.

To Chet's amusement, the Hardys relished the four hearty sandwiches as much as he.

"Wow! I must've been hungry!" Joe chuckled.

A short time later they were en route again. Suddenly Joe exclaimed, "I smell something burning. Whew!" The next instant he cried, "Pull over, Frank! Quick!"

Frank swerved the big car onto the shoulder. It lurched to a stop. "Look in the back!" Joe shouted. "The dynamite!"

To their horror, a crude string fuse, inserted into the box, was sputtering up to the lid. Joe leaped over the seat, yanked the string, and flung it from the car.

"I *thought* I heard a car slow up while we were eating," he said grimly. "But it never came into view."

"It probably dropped someone off," Frank reasoned. "He could have put in that fuse, work-

ing on the road side of the convertible to keep
out of our sight."

"He waited until he saw us coming back," Joe
added. "Then he lighted the fuse and slipped
into the woods across the road."

"Yes. Where his pal in the car will pick him up
again," Frank concluded. "Remember, everybody
in Larchmont knew we'd gone to Dobbsville for
the explosive. Some of the gang followed us, although there was no car in back of us before we
parked."

Shaken, the boys went on. Soon they were speed-
ing along the fishermen's road toward their camp.

Here they encountered the tall figure of Professor Rand pacing nervously up and down. "I'm
so excited, I couldn't sit at home and wait!" he
confessed.

"We're all set. Operation Dynamite's under
way!" Joe announced.

In a matter of minutes the small procession
headed for the pond. Chet toted the rucksack of
diving gear. Professor Rand carried digging im-
plements and the metal detector. Frank and Joe
took turns carrying the box of dynamite.

At last they reached the water's edge. The professor had already concurred with the Hardys
that it would be best to attempt raising the chest
first. Later the boys would show him the place
where they had unearthed the Indian relics. "I
realize," he said, "that by now the gang knows

you lads have escaped their malicious trap. They may try something worse at any time."

The Hardys had just put on their underwater gear when Bart arrived. Then Frank opened the wooden case and checked the paper-wrapped sticks of dynamite.

"We'll rig one stick," he decided quickly. "It may be all we need. Besides, it's safer that way."

With Frank carrying the explosive, the brothers submerged. Joe swam ahead, cutting a path through the cypress roots. Frank followed, and carefully planted the charge near the base of the tree trunk, but at sufficient distance not to damage the chest. While Joe stood by, Frank took a blasting cap from his belt and quickly inserted it into the dynamite. He then connected the cap's wires to a battery. This done, the brothers struck out swiftly to the surface.

Swimming ashore, the Hardys led Rand, Worth, and Chet around the bank away from the blasting area. Frank checked his waterproof watch. "Any minute now."

Tensely the five stared at the placid waters.

"There she blows!" Joe sang out as a muffled rumble shook the ground. A sudden agitation showed on the water's surface as if a geyser had gushed up from below. A grotesque, clawlike root rose into the sunshine, then sank back into the muddy waters.

Anxiously the onlookers wondered if the ex-

plosive had freed the chest. "We'll let things settle down a bit," Frank advised.

When the water had cleared somewhat, many
old, long-submerged trees could be seen pushed
up into shallow water.

Frank and Joe, after another minute, plunged
in. Knifing downward, they darted nimbly between and under loosened logs and chunks of
rotted trees. To the impatient boys, the pond
seemed bottomless.

Determinedly the brothers sought out the site
of the ancient cypress. Eagerly they scanned the
muddy area, still churning from the blast. Simultaneously Frank and Joe spotted the square
wooden box protruding from the silt. They
tugged and finally lifted it out. The boys carried
it between them, as they swam to the surface.

On shore, Professor Rand leaped with excitement, while Chet gave a whoop of joy. Bart
Worth shouted, "Nice work, fellows!"

At last Frank and Joe placed the old chest
safely on the pond's bank. The professor grabbed
a hammer, ready to knock off the sturdy cypress
lock!

CHAPTER XIX

Sinister Absence

"WAIT!" Frank ordered. The boy placed one foot on the lid of the box. "Nobody opens this chest now!"

"Why not?" Bart Worth asked in amazement. "This is what we've all been working for!"

"Bart," Frank explained, "your libel suit is involved. The chest has been found on disputed ground. If we break the lock, Blackstone can claim we inserted the papers that prove your case."

"But Professor Rand is a witness!"

"Not a very good one, from the court's point of view," Frank answered. "He has a quarrel of his own with Blackstone, who could claim some of the money in the chest had been stolen. If we open the box now, both of you stand to lose what you want from it."

The professor seemed unwilling to take his hands from the valuable chest. "Surely the law will allow us at least to open it and look inside."

"It will," Frank assured him, "as long as we do so in Blackstone's presence. There's no other safe way."

"Frank's right," agreed Joe.

Although Professor Rand continued to protest, Bart Worth gave in with a sigh. "I see the point," he admitted. "After all, I don't want to damage my own evidence. But suppose the papers aren't there?" he added anxiously.

"We'll have to take that chance," Frank replied.

Soon the yellow convertible was heading back swiftly toward town. The cypress box rested on the front seat between Frank and Joe.

Accompanied by Bart and the professor, the boys carried the chest up to the *Record* office. Meantime, Chet ran off to the hardware store. Soon he returned with a new padlock, which Frank promptly snapped on the box, slipping the key into his pocket.

"Now, Bart," he asked, "will you open your safe and put the chest inside, please?"

Silently, the young editor complied. Then Frank picked up the telephone and called Blackstone's residence.

Everyone in Bart's little office was silent as Frank waited for an answer. Finally the receiver at the other end was picked up.

"Hello. This is Blackstone." The big man's voice sounded considerably weaker than usual.

"Mr. Blackstone, this is Frank Hardy," the boy began.

"Hardy—yes, yes, the young fellow who pulled me out of the water." The businessman hesitated, then added gruffly, "Have to thank you."

"Glad we could help, sir," Frank replied. "I have some news for you. We've found the chest which I believe contains your ancestor's hidden fortune and family records."

"Found it! Where?"

"At the bottom of the pond, this afternoon."

Instantly the merchant's tone grew aggressive. "You must have trespassed on my property. If you've opened that box, or taken anything from it, I'll have the law on you!"

"Don't worry. We haven't opened it," Frank told him calmly. "The box has just been placed in a safe here at the *Record* office. A new padlock has been put on. I assure you the chest won't be opened until you're here to watch. How soon can you come, sir?"

Blackstone's voice faltered. "Look here, I—I'm still a bit shaky from the close call I had. My doctor insists I can't leave the house for another day."

"Tomorrow night, then?"

"At nine-thirty," Blackstone agreed.

Frank went on, "A disinterested person will

stay at the office until then to guarantee that nobody tampers with the chest."

As soon as Frank had hung up, Bart protested hotly, "I wouldn't dream of tampering."

"I know," Frank calmed him. "But we must give Mr. Blackstone a safeguard, so he can't dispute your evidence later."

"Who's this 'disinterested person'?" Chet spoke up suspiciously.

Frank and Joe simply grinned at him.

"Oh, no!" the stout boy protested. "All day and all night I have to stay in this little office?"

"You'll learn the newspaper trade," Joe told him.

"Sure, sure. What will *you* two be doing all this time?" Chet demanded.

"First," Frank replied, "we'll show Professor Rand where the Indian village is. We'll be back here about nine-thirty to keep you company."

"That's better," Chet said, mollified.

At a signal from the Hardys, Bart Worth lifted out a cardboard box from behind his desk and set it on top.

"Here's a treasure you *can* open," he said to Professor Rand.

The others stood by smiling as the professor undid the wrapping and examined with delight the Indian artifacts unearthed by the boys.

"Excellent! Marvelous specimens!" he exulted. "I'd like to see the Indian site right away!"

Accordingly, Frank, Joe, and Rand left the building. Rand climbed into the convertible, but suddenly Frank remembered something. "We'll need a good rake for sifting."

The brothers hurried up the street to the hardware store. Several minutes later they came out with the tool. At the same time, the boys saw a familiar figure leaning over the convertible door. He was carrying on a heated discussion with Rand.

"Cutter!" Joe exclaimed, and the Hardys hurried forward.

"No, no," the professor was saying in a loud voice. "I'll positively not sell my rights to the pond. *Especially* not now. That's final!"

Cutter's face took on an ugly look. Before the Hardys could reach him, he caught sight of the boys. He ran down the street, and disappeared around the corner.

"Let's go after him!" Joe urged. "I want to ask him a few questions about his partners, Stewart and Jed!"

Frank held his brother back. "We'll catch up with him later, after we keep our promise to the professor."

As they drove toward the beach camp, Joe said casually, "Sounded like Cutter was offering to buy your claim to the pond, Professor Rand."

The gangling scholar nodded impatiently. "Yes. He wants to make it into a fishing club, or some such nonsense. The man's an infernal nuisance! Just another of Samuel's hirelings."

"That's funny," Frank mused. "Mr. Blackstone thinks Cutter's working for you, and you think he's working for Blackstone. And he gave both of you the same line about the fishing club."

The professor looked up, startled. "What! How do you know that?" he demanded sharply.

"We overheard Cutter try to buy Mr. Blackstone's rights," Frank explained. "Your cousin gave him a final No, and a shaking besides. That was the same night Mr. Blackstone was dragged into the pond!"

"You suggest *I* should be afraid of that pest Cutter?" asked Rand with contempt. "Absolute nonsense. I have one enemy in the world: Samuel Blackstone. Even he wouldn't go so far as to—er—harm me, either with his henchman's help or without it."

The boys did not mention having seen Blackstone strike Rand. But Frank said, "Someone else might—the person who nearly drowned Mr. Blackstone."

"Samuel should keep away from the water," Rand stubbornly retorted. "He always thinks somebody's out to get him."

They had no sooner reached the camp than, to the Hardys' great surprise, Rand asked them to drive him home.

"I *do* want to see the Indian site," explained

the professor in some agitation. "But—well, I want to explore it without interruption. If we go there now, this fellow Cutter might show up and start badgering me about the land. I'll meet you boys by the pond tonight, at seven-thirty. We'll go then."

Shrugging, the Hardys agreed, and took the scholar to his house. "Be on your guard," Frank warned him.

It was just seven-thirty when Frank and Joe, equipped with digging tools, arrived at the pond. They also carried diving gear, in case they should need it.

"Professor Rand!" Joe called out.

There was no reply. The boys waited. The sun sank lower. Presently bullfrogs began croaking from the pond and deep within the swamp. Still the tall man did not arrive.

When almost an hour had elapsed, the young detectives felt a twinge of concern. What was delaying the professor? He had been so eager to visit the Indian spot.

"Maybe he's at home and forgot the time," Joe said hopefully. "I'll check."

He made his way up toward the old house. But in a few minutes he returned alone.

"I called and knocked," Joe reported. "No answer."

A sudden thought crossed Frank's mind. "Suppose the professor was so eager he came early," he suggested.

"And the same thing happened to him as happened to Blackstone!" Joe finished.

Feverishly the boys stripped off their clothes and donned their flippers, lungs, and face masks. Then Frank took an underwater light in one hand and submerged.

He swam steadily along the pond's shore line. His light showed up the usual stones and sunken trees, but no trace of the missing professor. Frank turned and worked back deeper along the bottom.

Joe stood waiting tensely as the moon climbed over the swamp trees. Finally Frank's head popped above the surface and he stood up in the shallows.

"What luck?" Joe called. "Did you—"

But horror choked off the words. A dark, slithery creature had loomed out of the water behind his brother. Now, with sharp fins glistening and fantastic head waving from side to side, it advanced on the unsuspecting Frank.

"Look out!" Joe shrieked. The next moment something struck him on the back of his head, and he fell, unconscious.

Just as Frank whirled, the monstrous creature sprang upon him.

CHAPTER XX

Feud's End

Slowly Joe opened his eyes. He found himself lying on the floor of a small room. The boy thought he must be dizzy from the blow, for he felt a rocking motion. Then he became aware of a soft lapping noise and sat up gingerly.

Despite his throbbing head, Joe's keen eyes took in his surroundings. A dim light was burning in the room. In one wall were two round windows.

"A boat's cabin!" he thought.

Somebody groaned beside him. Frank raised himself up and shook his head. "Where are we?"

"Wish I knew," Joe answered.

Frank made a face. "From the smell, I'd say we're in the fishing boat Cutter's been using to spy on us. Say! Professor Rand is here too!"

A long, angular figure on the floor beneath the portholes stirred, then sat up also. The professsor blinked at the Hardy boys in bewilderment.

"Are you all right?" Joe asked him.

"Yes—I think so, considering I was struck on the head."

"I was conked, too," said Joe. He turned to his brother. "Did that monster knock you out?"

"Must have," Frank replied. "Last thing I remember is when it grabbed me. Hmm. I wonder—"

Frank crawled over to a black foot locker with a pool of water spreading out from it.

"I thought so," he muttered, peering inside.

The boy pulled out a large black rubber diving suit, with a sharp serrate fin and enormous rubber head attachment!

"Here's our 'monster'!" he announced. "I thought I smelled rubber when it got me."

"Some costume!" Joe exclaimed wryly. "But who was wearing it?"

"*I* was!" came a voice from the doorway.

"Mr. Cutter!" gasped the professor.

The tall, pale man sneered at them as he entered the cabin. "Better come down, Jed," Cutter called. "The prisoners are awake."

A moment later the burly, flat-faced man shuffled into the cabin. "You kids won't be so cocky after this!" Jed rasped triumphantly.

The Hardys kept cool heads. Now Frank said, "Why not tell us your real scheme, Cutter, since we're your prisoners?"

The erstwhile antique dealer answered readily. "I'm after the Blackstone fortune, too. Read about it in a book of lost American treasures. The money, plus the *main* value of the pond, make it a desirable body of water!"

"Main value," Joe repeated. "You mean for your fishing resort?"

"Won't tell you *that*." Cutter laughed. "But thanks for raising the buried chest. One of my helpers saw you carry it into the *Record* office and heard you make that nine-thirty date. Through him, too, I kept constant track of you three, your fat friend, Worth, and Blackstone.

"I made up my 'monster' suit to search the pond and frighten away any curious intruders," he went on. "That included you Hardys the night I made my second dive. See this rope with the weights on both ends? That's what I used to drag Blackstone into the water. By the way, I was a printer by trade. I managed to sneak into the *Record* office's composing room and insert the extra bit in Worth's story. Thought I'd make Blackstone so tired of the pond he'd be glad to sell.

"And now," the man said, as he flashed a self-satisfied smile, "I'm on Easy Street. You've done it. At nine-thirty tomorrow night, Stewart, Jed, and I go to that meeting at Worth's office, settle Blackstone, tie up your friends, and come out with the money!"

"What happens to us?" Joe demanded tersely.

"By then you'll all be out of the picture—permanently. With Rand here, and Blackstone gone, I'll buy up the pond area. Neither man has heirs. The executors will be glad to sell."

"Guess again," Joe retorted defiantly. "Chet will miss us and think of this boat!"

"Let him," said Cutter. "We're far from our usual anchoring place. Stewart has sent a note to Bart Worth, supposedly from you Hardys, that you're in a nearby town and will be back for the meeting."

"So Stewart's the one who did the other phony notes," Joe broke in.

Cutter nodded. "Too bad they didn't work, and that you escaped when we 'fixed' the plane, and lit the dynamite fuse in your car; also at the lighthouse—that was Jed and Stewart's job. You were lucky getting out of Rand's house before Jed and I returned. But this time we'll be very thorough!"

For the remainder of the night and into the following day, Frank, Joe, and Professor Rand sat on the cabin floor. They were given only a little water and stale bread. Desperately the boys waited for a break. But their guards were vigilant. At noon, and again as the light faded outside, the captors spelled one another for meals.

"Okay, Jed," Cutter signaled later that evening. "Get busy!"

The powerful man left the cabin. Soon the boys heard several sharp, splintering blows. "All set!" called the hoarse voice.

"Good-by. Enjoy yourselves!" said Cutter pleasantly, as he stepped out and locked the cabin door.

In a few minutes the three captives heard the put-put of a motorboat.

"The gang's pulled out and we're not even tied up!" Joe exclaimed.

Simultaneously the cabin tilted over to one side. "The boat's sinking!" Frank cried out. "That's why! They mean to drown us and destroy the evidence!"

The Hardys' minds raced for a way out of their predicament. One chance occurred to Frank. "Help me with this foot locker, Joe!" he cried.

The brothers swung the heavy chest with all their strength at the door, so that its sharp corner smashed through the wood. Joe reached through the jagged hole and turned the lock.

The Hardys, followed by Professor Rand, rushed up on deck. Here they found sea water filling the afterpart of the vessel.

"I can't swim!" cried Professor Rand.

"I have a plan," Frank assured him. "Joe, take the fire axe and knock loose whatever pieces of wood you can."

Frank, meanwhile, ran to the cabin, now ankle-deep in water, and returned with a bottle of rub-

Soon the ocean was pouring over the gunwales
of the sinking boat

bing alcohol. On deck, where the gang had apparently eaten, was an opened five-pound box of sugar.

As Joe whacked off the big chunks of wood, Frank sprinkled them with sugar and saturated them with alcohol. As he worked, the boy asked the professor to ignite the pieces.

Feverishly Rand struck one match after another. As the wood flared up, Joe slid the eerie, green-burning floats onto the dark surface of the sea.

"Hope somebody spots them," Joe said tensely. "It's our only chance, and maybe Chet's!"

Soon the ocean was pouring over the gunwales of the sinking boat. Joe launched his last green flare. The boys heaved the cabin door overboard, and plunged after it with Professor Rand. Behind them, the fishing smack settled quickly below the sea.

"Hold on to the door, Professor," Frank directed. "Joe and I will stay on either side of you. All we can do now is wait."

The strange, green-flaming floats bobbed all around them. Stars twinkled overhead. Suddenly Joe sighted red and yellow lights moving in the distance. As the vessel drew closer, he shouted in relief, "Coast Guard!"

Soon the long, trim cutter bore down on them, its powerful searchlight sweeping the water.

"Ahoy!" shouted a crewman. "We'll drop a ladder. Hang on."

Within minutes the exhausted trio had been hauled aboard.

"Larchmont!" Frank gasped. "We must get there right away. It's a matter of life or death!"

The cutter plowed through the water at full speed. As it glided alongside the dock at Larchmont, Frank, Joe, and Rand leaped over the side and set out at a dead run for the town square. Frank's watch showed nine-thirty!

The three raced along the sidewalk toward the newspaper office. As they reached it, a car sped up and screeched to a stop.

"Get them!" called a firm voice.

Two men jumped from the automobile and grabbed the Hardys. "Police!" cried Joe. "What—?"

"Frank! Joe!" came a familiar voice behind them. "You here, and all right?"

"Dad!" burst out the astounded brothers as Fenton Hardy stepped forward.

"It's okay," he said to the officers. "These are my sons."

"We've no time to lose, Dad!" said Frank. Briefly, he brought his father up to date. With revolvers drawn, the men followed as Frank and Joe tiptoed upstairs.

They were just in time to see four masked men

backing away from Bart Worth's office! One, a brawny, broad-shouldered fellow, carried the cypress chest. The tall, thin leader was in the doorway, his pistol leveled at Samuel Blackstone!

Frank and Joe dived forward and brought the armed man to the floor. A shot rang out. A bullet whacked into the ceiling. Then Joe tore off the fellow's mask. Henry Cutter lay glaring at them. The other thugs turned to flee.

"Drop your weapons!" Fenton Hardy ordered crisply. "You're covered. You there—put down that chest!"

Chet, Bart, and Blackstone rushed from the office.

"You got my SOS, Mr. Hardy!" cried Chet. "I knew when Bart showed me that note it wasn't from Frank and Joe!"

Quickly the policemen unmasked Cutter's henchmen. They proved to be Jed, Stewart, and the man the Hardys had seen catching alligators. The prisoners were handcuffed and led away.

"How *did* you get here so fast, Dad?" Frank asked.

"Fortunately I got a reservation on a jet from Jamaica as soon as I got Chet's wire," the detective explained.

The Hardys clapped their stout friend gratefully on the back, and the others thanked all three boys for the rescue.

Now Samuel Blackstone stepped forward. "I

wish to settle the matter of the chest. Remember, whatever is in it belongs to the Blackstone family."

"Not at all," Rand returned hotly. "The money was made by smuggling through Hidden Harbor, which is at least partly my property!"

Blackstone thundered, "Ruel, you'll find yourself up against a slander suit if you insinuate that my side of the family was dishonest!"

"They *were* smugglers of pirate goods!" the professor insisted vehemently.

Bart Worth spoke up. "Open the chest. If the papers *are* there, you won't be suing anybody, Mr. Blackstone."

Frank quickly opened the locks and raised the lid, disclosing another, smaller chest. Unlatching this, the boy untied a cloth pouch and opened it.

"Money!" Chet whooped. "Millions!"

Mr. Blackstone and Professor Rand both reached for the bag. "Mine!" they cried together.

Suddenly an odd expression crossed Frank's face. He held up one of the packages of bills. "Confederate States of America," he read slowly.

A stunned silence followed. Wordlessly, Frank and Joe removed the stacks of worthless Civil War bills. Then Frank drew out a flat oilskin envelope. Inside was a leather book. Swiftly the boy leafed through the pages.

"Well?" Bart Worth asked tensely. "What does it say?"

Frank looked up. "Everything: dates, amounts, and prices for stolen goods received from pirate ships at Hidden Harbor. Look for yourself, Mr. Blackstone."

The big man quietly took the ledger. His face darkened as he read the notations. His aggressive manner disappeared.

"I'm a proud man," he admitted in a low voice. "I've always suspected this was true, but I—I couldn't admit it, even to myself." He turned to Worth. "I apologize to you, sir. Of course, I'll cancel my suit."

"So there was no treasure in the pond after all," Rand concluded sadly.

"Yes," Frank said unexpectedly, "there is!"

Everyone stared at him in disbelief. "What do you mean?" Chet asked.

Frank's amazing announcement came as a surprise to Chet. He had been deep in thought wondering when he would be involved with the Hardys in another mystery. Sooner than he expected, **THE SINISTER SIGNPOST** was to be their next challenge.

In answer to Chet's question, Frank said, "When I was searching for Professor Rand in the pond last night, I noticed that all the trees exposed by the blasting were cypress. Most of them have stood there for centuries, and will bring a huge fortune in valuable wood—to persons who can get it out and market it!"

"So *that's* what Cutter meant!" Joe exclaimed. "The cypress is the pond's 'main value'!"

Frank nodded, and turned to the cousins. "You know where your treasure is." He smiled. "You'll both profit from it by working together."

"I have some money," Blackstone objected, "but not enough for a project this size. Besides, I don't think I could work with Ruel as a partner."

"Same here!" snapped Rand.

"Try this idea," Fenton Hardy suggested suddenly. "My client in Jamaica deals in valuable lumber. He'd like to branch out in this country, and I know he'd make a third partner for you both. He would contribute the necessary capital, but not unless you two settle your squabble."

"I've no money," Professor Rand said thoughtfully, "but we *could* build the working plant on my land, and I'd give my home over for business offices. But the Indian village must be excavated first. State University will certainly finance it, when they see what the Hardy boys have dug up!"

"Well—" grumbled Blackstone, "all right. But I'll bet we can't work together!"

"You can *make* the deal work," Bart spoke up. "Don't forget, Frank and Joe saved both your lives. The least you can do is make peace."

"That's so," Blackstone admitted.

Silently, he reached across and shook Rand's outstretched hand. The old feud was over. Hidden Harbor had given up its secret!

ORDER FORM

HARDY BOYS MYSTERY SERIES
by Franklin W. Dixon

57 TITLES AT YOUR BOOKSELLER OR COMPLETE AND MAIL THIS HANDY COUPON TO:

GROSSET & DUNLAP, INC.
P.O. Box 941, Madison Square Post Office, New York, N.Y. 10010

Please send me the Hardy Boys Mystery and Adventure Book(s) checked below @ $2.95 each, plus 25¢ *per book* postage and handling. My check or money order for $_____ is enclosed.

☐	1. Tower Treasure	8901-7	☐	28. The Sign of the Crooked Arrow	8928-9
☐	2. House on the Cliff	8902-5	☐	29. The Secret of the Lost Tunnel	8929-7
☐	3. Secret of the Old Mill	8903-3	☐	30. Wailing Siren Mystery	8930-0
☐	4. Missing Chums	8904-1	☐	31. Secret of Wildcat Swamp	8931-9
☐	5. Hunting for Hidden Gold	8905-X	☐	32. Crisscross Shadow	8932-7
☐	6. Shore Road Mystery	8906-8	☐	33. The Yellow Feather Mystery	8933-5
☐	7. Secret of the Caves	8907-8	☐	34. The Hooded Hawk Mystery	8934-3
☐	8. Mystery of Cabin Island	8908-4	☐	35. The Clue in the Embers	8935-1
☐	9. Great Airport Mystery	8909-2	☐	36. The Secrets of Pirates Hill	8936-X
☐	10. What Happened At Midnight	8910-6	☐	37. Ghost at Skeleton Rock	8937-8
☐	11. While the Clock Ticked	8911-4	☐	38. Mystery at Devil's Paw	8938-6
☐	12. Footprints Under the Window	8912-2	☐	39. Mystery of the Chinese Junk	8939-4
☐	13. Mark on the Door	8913-0	☐	40. Mystery of the Desert Giant	8940-8
☐	14. Hidden Harbor Mystery	8914-9	☐	41. Clue of the Screeching Owl	8941-6
☐	15. Sinister Sign Post	8915-7	☐	42. Viking Symbol Mystery	8942-4
☐	16. A Figure in Hiding	8916-6	☐	43. Mystery of the Aztec Warrior	8943-2
☐	17. Secret Warning	8917-3	☐	44. Haunted Fort	8944-0
☐	18. Twisted Claw	8918-1	☐	45. Mystery of the Spiral Bridge	8945-9
☐	19. Disappearing Floor	8919-X	☐	46. Secret Agent on Flight 101	8946-7
☐	20. Mystery of the Flying Express	8920-3	☐	47. Mystery of the Whale Tattoo	8947-5
☐	21. The Clue of the Broken Blade	8921-1	☐	48. The Arctic Patrol Mystery	8948-3
☐	22. The Flickering Torch Mystery	8922-X	☐	49. The Bombay Boomerang	8949-1
☐	23. Melted Coins	8923-3	☐	50. Danger on Vampire Trail	8950-5
☐	24. Short-Wave Mystery	8924-6	☐	51. The Masked Monkey	8951-3
☐	25. Secret Panel	8925-4	☐	52. The Shattered Helmet	8952-3
☐	26. The Phantom Freighter	8926-2	☐	53. The Clue of the Hissing Serpent	8953-X
☐	27. Secret of Skull Mountain	8927-0	☐	54. The Mysterious Caravan	8954-8
			☐	55. The Witchmaster's Key	8955-6
			☐	56. The Jungle Pyramid	8956-4
			☐	57. The Firebird Rocket	8957-2

SHIP TO:

NAME _____
(please print)

ADDRESS _____

CITY _____ STATE _____ ZIP _____

Printed in U.S.A.   **Please do not send cash.**